THE END OF
LIEUTENANT
BORUVKA

THE END OF LIEUTENANT BORUVKA

BY JOSEF SKVORECKY

Translated by Paul Wilson

W · W · Norton & Company · New York · London

Printed in the United States of America.

The text of this book is composed in 10/13 Galliard, with display type set
in Woodcut. Composition and manufacturing by The Maple-Vail Book
Manufacturing Group

First Edition

Library of Congress Cataloging-in-Publication Data
Skvorecky, Josef.
[Konec poručíka Borůvky. English]
The end of Lieutenant Boruvka / Josef Skvorecky ; translated by
Paul Wilson.
p. cm.
Translation of: Konec poručíka Borůvky.
I. Title.
PG5038.S527K613   1990
891.8'635—dc20   89–34443

ISBN 0-393-02785-6

W. W. Norton & Company, Inc., 500 Fifth Avenue, New York, N. Y. 10110
W. W. Norton & Company Ltd., 37 Great Russell Street, London WC1B 3NU

1 2 3 4 5 6 7 8 9 0

Whenever you try to discover The People,
it always gets down to someone in the end.
John Dos Passos

Contents

Author's Note

In the few works of fiction written so far by Czech authors about the events of the year 1968 and their consequences, the heroes have invariably been intellectuals. In this collection of crime stories, however, I have tried to look at some of the causes and results of that bust-up of Marxism through the eyes of a simple man.

Some knowledge of the historical background is probably necessary if the reader is to understand the implications of the tales. Czechoslovakia was created in 1918, after the collapse of the Austro-Hungarian Empire. It lost its independence in March 1939—six months after the Munich Agreement—and suffered a brutal Nazi occupation from 1939 to 1945.

In 1948 the Communist Party grabbed power under Klement Gottwald and the country slipped under Russian domination, becoming a Soviet-style state; it endured twenty years of Marxism-Leninism, with its murders and its blatant injustice masked as "class justice," its Newspeak and its new class of the "more equal among equals."

But in 1968 Czechoslovakia blossomed during an eight-month

period when Alexander Dubcek replaced the hard-line Stalinist Antonin Novotny as Party leader. In this period, known as the "Prague Spring," the country went through an experience which, in most respects, was identical to what is currently going on in the Soviet Union under Gorbachev: past crimes of the regime were revealed, censorship was abolished, market-oriented economic reforms were planned, the possibility of reintroducing the prewar multi-party system was discussed, and so on.

These efforts came to an abrupt end on August 21, 1968, when half a million troops (mostly Soviet) and five thousand assault vehicles invaded the country. Dubcek and members of his leadership were flown to Moscow in shackles, and only barely escaped the fate of the Hungarian leader Imre Nagy, who was shot by the Soviets after the similar defeat of the Hungarian revolution in 1956.

This Attila-the-Hun intervention was described by the aggressors as the "Entry of the Fraternal Armies rendering Brotherly Help to the Czechs and Slovaks"—a falsification that is still accepted by the Gorbachev regime and seems to be officially regarded as the only thing the otherwise reprobate Brezhnev did right.

In the wake of this ambush, Czechoslovak citizens were subjected to a degrading Orwellization of their lives—called "normalization"—which was aimed at forcing these once free and truly democratic people into utter obedience and demoralization. On both points, the government almost succeeded: were it not for a handful of courageous and righteous men and women, Czechoslovakia would by now have been irrevocably crushed.

The five stories in this book are all loosely based on actual cases.

April 1989   J.S.

THE END OF LIEUTENANT BORUVKA

Miss Peskova Regrets

Lieutenant Boruvka had never said he believed in omens. But he was uneasy that Sunday—August 17, 1967—when he was awakened by a record player belonging to his daughter, Zuzana, playing a melancholy song into the sunny morning:

> Miss Otis regrets she's unable to
>   lunch today,
> Madam, Miss Otis regrets she's unable to
>   lunch today,
> She's sorry to be delayed
> But last evening down in Lover's Lane she
>   strayed,
> Madam, Miss Otis regrets she's unable to
>   lunch today.

The lieutenant had no idea who Miss Otis was or why she couldn't keep her appointment. On the other hand, he suspected that Zuzana was not playing the song purely because she liked the music, and the thought made him gloomy.

"Madam . . . ," sang the bard in a whiskey baritone, and the lieutenant's moon-shaped face wrinkled in a frown. Suddenly the wailing of a baby joined the baritone. Lying in bed, the old detective grew even sadder. His aversion to singers with manly voices was one point of a triangle whose remaining apexes were a squalling child and a young man called Mack. That was his real name, not a nickname. The young man was not the baby's father, but it was the lieutenant's fervent hope that he soon would be—which was why Zuzana's interest in vocalists bothered him. He knew her weakness for pop singers. To him it seemed undiminished even now that she had become a mother, and he was afraid Mack's present willingness to become the child's father might evaporate in the heat of jealousy. So far, only Zuzana and the lieutenant knew the biological father's identity. Mrs. Boruvka stubbornly continued to believe in the paternity of Olda Spacek, who wore snazzy clothes and was a stunt pilot in the Army Aeronautics Club. Rather than reveal the truth to her mother, Zuzana preferred playing the role of Spacek's cast-off mistress (or "slut," in moments when Mrs. Boruvka was particularly upset and her Italian blood came to a boil) and absolutely refused to sue the pilot for child support, something her pride would not allow her to do.

> When she woke up and found that her dream
>   of love was gone,
> Madam, she ran to the man who had led her so far
>   astray. . . .

A fresh Sunday-morning breeze was blowing through the living room, and the old detective was overpowered by a premonition. He knew that this shouldn't be allowed to happen, that he ought to put it resolutely out of his mind as an irrational and therefore unscientific habit of thought. The trouble was that premonitions were so often right. Years before, for instance, when he had learned the name of the then-new chief of the Homicide Division, he had been overcome by that same inappropriate feeling which, although unscientific, had proved accurate. During Captain D'Eath's brief career (originally a barber, then a zealous Party member, D'Eath had come to Homicide from the post of director of Prague radio because he refused to use a pseudonym) there had been a rush of people who had taken it upon themselves to deprive their fellow human beings of life. With the exception of one case, which Captain D'Eath had personally supervised, the perpetrators had all been run to ground by Lieutenant Boruvka, and had ultimately been deprived of their own lives in a way the old detective considered medieval and unworthy of modern penology. Each time this had happened, it had cost him many sleepless nights. He never went to watch an execution, although he had the right to do so and Sergeant Malek even claimed that it was his official duty—a duty the sergeant himself was only too glad to carry out.

The leading Party journal, whose sports section the lieutenant read every day, usually characterized the punishment as "just," sometimes qualified by the phrase "harsh but." The old detective had no doubts whatever about its harshness, but he was less certain about the justice of it. He lacked philosophical arguments against the penalty, and the punishment was even acceptable to his religion—which the venerable Father Meloun had once driven so thoroughly into his round head, back in the Kostelec high school, that, although he had long since stopped going to church out of simple political caution, the lieutenant had never been able to shake the feeling that God existed after all. What the lieutenant could never understand was why God allowed things to happen that filled him with such doubt.

The aptness of the captain's name was finally confirmed by an execution that put an end to D'Eath's personal involvement in the art of detection. At the time the lieutenant had refused to believe the clues; they were too blatant and too inconclusive. But they appealed to the captain because they suggested a politically motivated murder. The victim had been a member of the Communist Party, and some trails vaguely led to a member of the Catholic People's Party—now reduced to the political status and influence of the Cat-Lovers' Club. But the lieutenant had refused to attribute to a Catholic ways of thinking that were more proper to the allegedly Marxist persuasion of the victim, and so Captain D'Eath had taken him off the case. Before the lieutenant, working unofficially in his off hours, had managed to track down the real killer, D'Eath had brought the case to the point where the harshest available punishment was applied to the wrong person. The real offender turned out to be a member of no political party, who had killed the Communist (a former goldsmith) not out of class hatred but merely to get his hands on some jewelry the man had stashed away when his shop was nationalized. When he too met his harsh and, in his case, arguably just punishment—after the Party Department of Justice had sorted out some legal problems concerning two death sentences in a case involving only one murder and one murderer—the department had transferred Captain D'Eath to the Secret Police, where, over his protests, they made him change his name to Sedlacek (one of two service pseudonyms—the other was Prochazka—routinely assigned to new members of that secretive outfit), and promoted him to major. The lieutenant took sick leave and went off to Kostelec. It was only after a week of wandering in the woods, and several nights (when no one would see him) standing vigil over the grave of an insignificant parish priest, that he felt strong enough to go back to Prague and face his job.

Why hadn't he thrown in the towel long ago? He didn't know. He was not by nature a philosophical man, and his logical abilities were bound up exclusively with concrete matters: fingerprints, ballistic reports, holes poked in carefully falsified alibis, contradictions uncovered in statements. Perhaps he stuck to his job because they paid him well, perhaps because it was his only real skill. By now he was too large of girth to be any good at his original profession, teaching physical education. And besides, he always felt even sorrier for the victims of murder than he did for the murderers. When he thought about this emotional distinction, he realized that this too was the influence of the parish priest from Kostelec. Death, the venerable Father Meloun had always said, finds convicted murderers less unprepared than their victims.

But not even that would have been enough to make the lieutenant remain with the Homicide squad. There was something else. It was a gift, something he could not explain, not even to himself. An irrepressible urge to get at the truth.

He pulled the pillow over his head to muffle the sound of the music, and the premonition that was spoiling the brisk Sunday morning grew annoyingly stronger. Then the telephone beside the bed rang. He picked it up.

"Josef!" said the voice of Sergeant Malek. "Sorry to interrupt your Sunday siesta, but we've got a suicide here. I know you're not on duty today, but you may remember this girl, so I thought—"

"Who is it?" asked the lieutenant sadly.

"Her name's Alena Peskova."

. . .

On his way to the site of the suicide, the lieutenant thought about the sad dancer. A crooked prosecutor named Hynais had once tried to blackmail her into going to bed with him. The girl's younger brother had just committed the crime of breaking some furniture at a rock concert; his status as a university student was in jeopardy, and Hynais got the case. He even got him acquitted, but before he was able to collect his reward his wife killed him. The lieutenant solved the case and the unruly rock 'n' roller was assigned to another prosecutor, who asked for an exemplary punishment of three years in a correction camp, and got it.

The smell of gas was still in the air when the lieutenant arrived at the scene, where Sergeant Malek and old Doctor Seifert were waiting for him. The gas had come from a stove in one corner of the small, cold, bachelor flat. The smell had been so overpowering that a neighbor, Mr. Vavra, a championship diver, noticed it at eight o'clock that morning, when he was leaving for a workout at the Barrandov pool. He put his nose to the keyhole, became alarmed, and started pounding on the door. When the dancer did not open up, he ran at the door with all his strength. It gave way and he flew inside. He saw at once what had happened. He shut off the gas, opened the window, called an ambulance, and until it arrived he very conscientiously performed artificial respiration on the girl. To no avail. The doctor who came with the ambulance crew pronounced her dead, then called the police.

She was lying on her back on a couch. She wore a short evening dress and her skin was white, as white as chalk. There was a bottle of wine on a tiny coffee table, almost empty. Beside it stood a glass with some wine still in it. She did not drink for joy, thought the lieutenant. A lonely drinker. He looked around. A saucepan stood on the stove; the milk in it had boiled over and extinguished the flame. It was a classic case.

The lieutenant looked around once more. The bachelor flat was modestly furnished, but he could see signs everywhere of that gentle person who had once been willing to save her brother's university career by paying the price women have paid since the days of ancient Babylon. And now she was lying here poisoned by gas. The lieutenant's eyes wandered over the sad flowers in a ceramic vase, over the picture of a long, reclining nude (he had no idea that it was a reproduction of a Modigliani), over the small bookshelf with several volumes published by the Friends of Poetry Club and the Readers' Club. He shook his head to rid himself of memories of the dead girl's past and went back to surveying the scene of the tragic accident. The dancer was still wearing one of her evening shoes. The other one had fallen off and was lying on the carpet like a sad, abandoned thing.

Something green was clinging to the bottom of the slender high heel. He bent over and picked the shoe up off the rug. The green thing was a wilted but still fresh four-leaf clover.

· · ·

The lieutenant's first impulse was to telephone some of the dancers he knew from the Odeon Theatre, but then he had second thoughts—thoughts that again smacked of premonition. He decided to wait for the results of the autopsy. Monday he spent investigating a murder: the perpetrator had hit his demonstrably unfaithful wife across the face with the flat of his hand so clumsily that she fell and cracked the back of her head on the corner of a metal kitchen table. Love and remorse had immediately triumphed over jealousy and the husband had turned himself in. The lieutenant liked cases like this. Although they too ended in punishments that were just, they were not of the "harsh but" variety.

. . .

A few minutes before the end of his shift Dr. Seifert came in.

"I don't know what to think, Josef," he said. "We're going to have to send this one over to psychiatry. I don't have the experience to deal with it."

The lieutenant looked at him blankly.

"That gal had a real potpourri of poisons in her," said the gray-haired doctor cynically. "In the first place, she was completely plastered, but not enough to make it alcohol poisoning. And then she also had a little gas in her lungs, but not enough to explain the exitus either. And thirdly—and maybe you'd better sit down for this one—"

"What is it?" said the lieutenant gloomily.

"LSD," said the doctor.

"What?"

"You heard me right the first time. LSD. Short for lysergic acid diethylamide."

The old detective had never heard of this before. "What's that?" he asked innocently.

"And you with a nineteen-year-old daughter, Josef? You're really out of touch. Ah well." Dr Seifert sighed and scratched his bald spot. "I can't keep up with it all myself. I'm not sure what benefits this wonder drug bestows. We're going to have to bring the shrinks in on this one; they work with this stuff. But Josef—where could she get LSD in Prague?"

"Karel, what *is* it?"

Dr. Seifert gave the out-of-touch detective as much explanation as he could. "In my opinion," he concluded, "there are only two possibilities. Either she got it from some irresponsible shrink, or else the girl got mixed up with Western tourists."

. . .

The lieutenant wondered most about the possibility of an irresponsible psychiatrist. He knew psychiatrists. Not professionally, exactly, but one of them had dated Zuzana, who at the time was battling a tendency to be rather full in the midriff—a tendency the detective mistakenly thought she had inherited from her father. Her main weapon in this struggle was basketball, but while it got her on the national team as a second stringer, it also stimulated her appetite to the point where the tendency asserted itself even more. As far as the lieutenant was concerned, Zuzana was still slender; he could see nothing wrong with her figure. But his daughter's idol at the time was a model called Twiggy, and her own forty-seven-centimeter waist horrified her. Then a psychiatrist with the strange name of Dr. Arne S. Exer began coming around to see her, and the lieutenant saw in that name a sign that boded ill for the future. Zuzana thought her admirer's name was a good joke, and when her father expressed concern she declared, "Anyway, he's no worse that way than—" and she swallowed the rest.

"Than who?" asked her father sternly. "And in what way?"

"No one, really."

"You must have had someone in mind."

"I didn't, honest!"

"But you were about to compare him with somebody!"

"No, I wasn't. It's just that he falls pretty much inside the general norm. Oh, I know the norms are kind of loose these days, but don't worry about me, Dad, I can look after myself." Zuzana spoke with—as the near future was to prove—unfounded self-confidence. "After all, my own mother is an example of what happens if I don't, right?"

And that silenced the lieutenant. Not long before, his daughter had displayed another quality which he just as mistakenly assumed she had inherited from him, but which all the same did not please him. When Zuzana had filled out an application form to study physical education at the university, she had alertly noticed a minor discrepancy between the date on her birth certificate and the date on her parents' marriage license. Assuming moral probity on the part of her puritanical begetters, she calculated that she must have been born in the third month of pregnancy. In great glee she had announced her discovery to her father, who was less than delighted by her deductive abilities.

. . .

Shortly after their conversation about the psychiatrist with the inauspicious name, Zuzana suddenly lost a lot of weight. When the lieutenant submitted her cupboard to an illegal search, he found three empty glass tubes labeled Dex-Fenmetrazine, and in a decidedly old-fashioned approach to the problem he confronted Dr. Arne S. Exer with them. He got no satisfaction—the psychiatrist managed to persuade him that he had done nothing unscientific or illegal, and had strictly observed the dosage prescribed of "Ferry," as the stuff was popularly known among girls desiring to improve their waist measurements and melancholics trying to get some kick out of life.

But now that the pills had worked and Zuzana was fashionably slim, the charm of the shrink's erotic surname wore thin and the volatile (not to mention fickle) second-string pivot of the national team dumped the psychiatrist, despite his vigorous protestations. Not long after, however, Zuzana began to fill out again, mainly around the waist. In fact, she filled out to the point where she was finally compelled to postpone her credit course in the high jump, and the lieutenant became a grandfather without ever becoming a father-in-law.

It bothered him a lot, but he couldn't bring himself to be mean to his daughter; he did no more than put on several amateurish displays of paternal wrath, which were utterly unsuccessful. Next to appear on Zuzana's scene, which had always been fairly populous, was a lad called Mack, and for six months now he had been without a rival. The lieutenant's hopes for father-in-lawhood had brightened once again, and were so far still brightening.

. . .

Mack was a lanky young man with a narrow face and hair slightly longer than Zuzana's. He spoke Czech with the singsong intonation of Prague but otherwise he was a pure-blooded Yankee. His parents were a red-headed Irish couple from Tennessee, and Mr.

McLaughlin was a jazz trumpeter by profession. When the Korean War broke out he had decided to settle in Czechoslovakia rather than joining the American army. He had been informed by Czechoslovak officials, however, that foreigners were allowed to settle there only if they asked for political asylum. McLaughlin had therefore invented a story about how he was being persecuted in the U.S.A. (where he hadn't been since he was sixteen) by a senator whose name he mistakenly spelled in his declaration as MacArthur. (The Czechoslovak officials subsequently corrected the spelling for him.) For this invention he was given a good job in the Lucerna Bar orchestra.

Mack had been born in Copenhagen and had been three when his parents came to Prague. Zuzana met him at the health center, where she was attending classes in the Soviet method of painless childbirth. (After the birth, her obstetrician declared that he'd never heard such an athletic young mother scream so loudly.) Mack had come to the health center with a bruised eye which he had contracted during a students' discussion at the Primator pub. "The only reason he fell for me," Zuzana later confessed to her father, with characteristic openness, "was because his eyeball was so badly squeezed out of shape that he said everyone looked as skinny as worms and I was the only one who looked normal. I just hope he won't cool off when he eye gets back to normal."

He didn't, perhaps because by the time his eye recovered it no longer took an optical illusion to make Zuzana look normal. On the other hand, a baby carriage conspicuous to any eye had appeared. But that didn't seem to bother Mack. The lieutenant only hoped it would stay that way.

· · ·

As he was sitting in his television room late that afternoon, it occurred to Boruvka that he needn't wait until the next day for the verdict of the experts from the psychiatric clinic. He had remembered yet another shrink: an old friend from the Kostelec high school, who had played guitar in the band in which the lieutenant blew the tenor sax. Unlike the detective, who had miserably abandoned his youthful love, the psychiatrist remained faithful and still spent most of his free time strumming the guitar with an amateur band. The lieutenant persuaded himself (by looking through the keyhole) that what Zuzana and Mack were up to in the next room was changing his granddaughter Lucy's diapers. Putting aside all the apprehensions raised yet again by the voice singing about the seductive qualities of stardust, he set out to find Dr. Rus.

. . .

The doctor was sitting on the podium playing the guitar and his face, puffed from alcohol, wore an expression of absolute bliss. A Dixeland band was phrasing a slow tune and a singer in a sequin-covered dress was whispering into the microphone in a gently misty voice:

> When she woke up and found that her dream
>   of love was gone,
> Madam . . .

Although the song again filled the lieutenant with an evil premonition, he cheered up. He knew the singer. She was a well-traveled lady who had been young for quite some time, and she had given him the occasional anxious dream in which a grim-visaged Father Meloun appeared, raised his index finger at him in stern admonition, and pointed to a certain pair of stone tablets. Each time he had the dream the lieutenant made a mental promise to change his ways, then peered guiltily across the double bed at Mrs. Boruvka, who was sleeping the sleep of the just and the righteous. But the worth of such promises is well known, especially when they concern young women with wide-set gray eyes, attractive voices, and perfect pitch—charms that are irresistible to a musical man.

. . .

"It's dangerous stuff, no doubt about it. I've read of cases in the States where people have OD'd on LSD," said Dr. Rus during the intermission. The singer was burning with curiosity and pretending she wasn't. "Course it's a matter of debate. There was this American beatnik poet in Prague a while ago, and he praised the stuff to the skies, said it was the perfect cure for writer's block. Well, maybe it is. But if you have any suicidal tendencies at all, they pretty well have to tie you down to keep you from jumping out the window."

"Is that so?" said the lieutenant thoughtfully.

"And if you've got any manic tendencies, then they have to tie you down to keep others from going out the window—against their will."

They fell silent, then the lieutenant spoke.

"According to what you say, I might reconstruct it like this," and he looked gloomily from Dr. Rus to the singer, whose name was Eve Adam. As the lieutenant knew, she was an accomplished sleuth herself, although not by profession, and Dr. Rus was an old and trusted friend. The detective felt no compunction discussing the case of the sad dancer with them. "First she drank, most likely to drawn her sorrows, then she took LSD to cheer herself up. But it heightened her tendency to suicide, and—" He stopped abruptly.

"The milk," said the singer.

The lieutenant blushed and said shamefully, "You're right, Eve. It's not logical."

"I'll say it isn't! Since when do suicides try to arrange their departure so it looks like an accident? And if it was an accident—" The singer paused; a wrinkle appeared on her forehead, but she regained control of herself and the wrinkle disappeared. "She's boozed and doped to her eyeballs," she continued, musing, "and suddenly she gets a craving for warm milk? When I'm like that, the only craving I have is for pickled herring."

"Not just straight pickles?" asked Dr. Rus, with a specialist's interest.

"That means—" said the detective.

"Well, I'd say it means exactly *that!*" said the singer. "Foul play.

Besides, do you think she'd get sauced up all by herself, at home, and put on an evening gown for the occasion? I mean, have you ever heard of a girl wearing an evening gown at home, all by herself? Either she wears a dressing gown or—"

"Eve—I mean—" The lieutenant stole an uncertain glance at Dr. Rus; although the doctor was an old friend, he had never told him about his special relationship with the band's vocalist. "You're right, Miss Adam—"

"And that bit about the milk boiling over!" exclaimed his secret friend. "That kind of thing only happens to old-age pensioners. No way. She had someone there with her, and first he gets her drunk and then he doses her up with LSD, the combination turns out to be lethal, the guy gets scared and remembers how pensioners—"

"You're right again, Miss Adam," repeated the lieutenant. In fact, though, he had remembered something else, something that threw a slightly different light on the blonde's train of thought.

The four-leaf clover stuck to the stiletto heel.

. . .

He spent the rest of the evening reading through the dancer's correspondence. Here she proved to be outstandingly methodical, which made the detective's task easier. The letters were stored on the lower shelf of a small wardrobe, and were bound with ribbons of various colors and organized alphabetically. On the upper shelf the lieutenant found letters from the girl's mother in Svinne Lady, written on lined paper. Each of them, almost without exception, contained three pieces of information: news about the weather in Svinne Lady, a report on the brother's latest letter from jail, and an announcement that a food parcel would follow. There was the greatest variety on this last point, for the food reflected the time of year and the church holidays: muffins from the fall fair, sausages when they slaughtered the pig, dried fruit for Christmas, hot cross buns for Easter, and, in summer, blueberry pie. The lieutenant wondered who actually ate all those old-fashioned delicacies and concluded that, whoever it was, it was probably not the dancer—not just because a diet of tidbits from Mother would have ruined the slender figure so essential in her profession, but also because he had already read the other letters in the wardrobe.

There weren't many of them—after all, this was the age of the telephone—and they were extremely fragmentary. Nevertheless, from them he had learned a little about the dead dancer's love life. It had hardly been satisfying. Most of the letters were epistles of sentimental adieu, which inevitably contained some of the standard excuses: "I think we'll both be better off." "It's been great, let's stay friends." "I'd make a lousy husband; you deserve something better." One of these altruists had even ended his valedictory missive with a misquote from the work of a popular poet: "It was magnificent—but, alas, it brings too much heartbreak!" Only the altruist's memory had failed him—or perhaps his subconscious mind had got the upper hand—because in his farewell note the line appeared with a slight modification: "It was magnificent—but, alas, it brings too much heartburn!"

Images of the mother's pies, muffins, and sausages swam into the lieutenant's mind.

But it was the final packet of letters—just two of them—that caught his attention and upset him, because he knew the author of these billets-doux: he was also the author of a notorious novel which had at one time, at the suggestion of the authorities, been roundly attacked by all correctly thinking (or at least writing) critics, and in the end had been banned. The author was of the lieutenant's own generation, and his name was Josef Kopanec—Fuck-up Joe, they called him.

On the one hand the letters betrayed that Kopanec was a literary professional, on the other hand that he was the type of man Zuzana called a "wick-dipper"—for which she was scolded by her father. There were passages in them that disturbed the detective deeply.

Not that they were lewd; not at all. But in the first letter the writer promised "Ferry for his little girl," whereas the other—

written two months later—took the form of a sermon to the effect that there had been quite enough Ferries. The jocularly amorous style of the first epistle degenerated in the second into a diction that seemed straight out of a textbook on clinical pharmacology. This letter was three months old.

The lieutenant leaned back in his chair and gazed out of his office window at the statue of St. Sidonius. He recalled his own embarrassing conversation on the theme of "Ferry" with Dr. Arne S. Exer; he recalled the slim dancer with the chalk-like face. She certainly hadn't taken the pills for the same reason the full-bodied Zuzana had. He pondered the thin, wilted bundles of letters tied up in their colored ribbons. That was what she had used the pills for, he thought. A pang of regret—sentimental, perhaps, but human—caught at his heart.

Where did the notorious writer get the pills from in the first place? And was it just Ferry? Or other things too? He reached for the telephone, dialed a number, and waited.

The author was not at home.

.   .   .

Nor was he at home the next morning, before the lieutenant left for the cemetery.

The funeral was extremely sad. A tiny old lady in full costume from the Chod region was supported by a young man in black drainpipe trousers and a ducktail haircut. The pair stood out strangely against a group of young women in miniskirts and equipped with transparent plastic umbrellas. The rain trickled down the old lady's cheeks, mingling with her large tears, and tears flowed under the plastic umbrellas as well. Beneath the drumming rain-drops a young priest sang in a beautiful tenor voice.

> If Thou, O Lord, were to weigh our
> iniquities,
> Who, O Lord, would not be found wanting?

She might not, thought the sentimental lieutenant. Again he remembered a deceased public prosecutor, a ceramic vase full of flowers, those volumes from the Friends of Poetry Club, and the sad little stiletto-heeled shoe on the fiber mat, with the four-leaf clover stuck to it. He tried hard not to cry himself, but failed. So he raised his round face to the rain to hide his tears.

. . .

Later that afternoon he found Kopanec at the Congress of Writers' Union. When the detective showed his ID to the man at the door, the man looked at him with obvious distaste. This caused such moral turmoil in the lieutenant that for a moment he had to lean against the wall of the packed hall, unable to concentrate on what was going on. He had told the man clearly enough, he thought, that he was from the *criminal* branch, and he'd even raised his voice on the word "criminal." Perhaps he hadn't said it loudly enough. But, damn it all, how could the man at the door be such a fool? Didn't he know that officers from the other police force had already entered the hall, without showing anyone their ID's? And if they had shown anything, it would have been a Writers' Union card. For God's sake—wouldn't these people ever understand how things worked?

He looked back at the man, but the man avoided his eyes and instead stared intently towards the speaker's platform, where an author was reading a paper in an unsteady voice. Behind him sat several rows of writers, all of them probably famous. The lieutenant knew very little about literature, and he had no idea who the speaker was. Of all the faces on the platform he could recognize only one, and it belonged not to the writer he was looking for, but to Comrade Kral, the Communist Party secretary for cultural affairs. The lieutenant knew him because Kral had recently spoken at a political instruction course. But he'd already forgotten what Kral had talked about, and in any case he hadn't learned anything he had not already heard, and then instantly forgotten in dozens of similar courses before that. The lieutenant had a memory only for tangible things, and political instruction was generally about unreal things like the growth of socialist consciousness among the inmates of socialist correctional institutions.

The gloom that had settled over him thanks to the man at the door was not lifted by the presence of the Party secretary, so he tried to concentrate on what the perspiring writer was saying. He caught one sentence: "We have to realize," said the speaker, "that in the past twenty years not a single human problem has been solved in this country."

The lieutenant was not a philosopher. He wasn't quite sure what the speaker meant by the phrase "human problem," and he didn't like the Party secretary on the platform. Nevertheless, his sense of justice mutinied—or was it perhaps his sense of truth? He found himself saying sliently, "That doesn't sound right! Something at least must have been—" But his thoughts were interrupted by thunderous applause. He looked around and saw Kopanec a few feet in front of him, clapping furiously.

. . .

"It has come to our attention that you've been procuring some strictly controlled and unauthorized drugs for a certain young lady," the lieutenant was saying in his very official voice. The applause had quieted down and the famous writer had obeyed his curt order and followed him out to the lobby.

"Me?" said Kopanec. His astonishment was unconvincing, and he flushed.

"Yes, you!"

"Did you bust her—I mean, arrest her?"

"Unfortunately not," said the lieutenant. He looked straight into the writer's shifty eyes. "She's been murdered."

He had to resuscitate the author with a shot of hard liquor in the bar off the lobby. When the famous man was again capable of perceiving the world around him, the lieutenant added, "The stuff was mostly Dex-Fenmetrazine. But there may also have been something else. Something, shall we say, stronger. D'you see what I'm getting at?"

The author shook his head.

"The beatnik," said the lieutenant.

The writer looked at him, still not comprehending.

"The American poet," said the lieutenant, "who got himself elected Kral Majales, the King of the May, instead of you. You withdrew your candidacy in his favor."

The famous author turned red in the face. The detective remembered the affair very well: the traditional students' festivities at Charles University, the marrying off of the King of the May to the Queen of the May—

"I—I don't follow you," gasped the writer.

"He could have brought other drugs into the country with him. LSD, for instance. And you were in close touch with him."

"But he didn't give me any!" the author cried. "I didn't even ask him to! I'm not interested in that dreck! All we did was get drunk on Czech whiskey in my apartment. He wasn't used to such low quality, and he messed up my bathroom, but—no LSD! All I ever—" Suddenly he lowered his voice. "I'll admit it, lieutenant, I did get some Dex-Fenmetrazine for Alena. Some time ago. Speed, you know. But never anything else!"

It turned out that the author was unable to come up with an alibi for the fateful night. His story was that he had been feeling depressed so he had got drunk on Czech whiskey—his stomach being used to *that* dreck—all alone, at home. When he had felt the euphoria of intoxication fading, he had set out into the nocturnal streets. He had tried to keep the euphoria alive in a number of pubs whose names he couldn't remember, until at last he entered a state known as "blackout." Someone must have taken him home in that condition, because in the morning he had woken up in his own bed with no recollection of how he had got there.

"Why were you depressed?" asked the detective suspiciously.

"I've got writer's block."

The lieutenant was amazed. "But you publish book after book, and I hear the print runs are very large."

"That's just what I'm talking about," said the author gloomily. "Quality writing comes out in small print runs."

"I don't understand," said the detective. Before Kopanec could explain further, he asked, "Where were you yesterday evening and this morning?"

"Drunk again," said the famous author. "The telephone woke me up in the morning, but I was feeling so low I didn't bother answering it. Hang on a moment!" he exclaimed, brightening somewhat. "I remember one of the bars I was in on Saturday! The Odeon! The one next to the theater! They know me there, they'll vouch for me!" Then he hesitated. "Or was it yesterday evening?" he thought for a moment, then became despondent. "I'm sorry, I just don't know. I don't know anything any more. Not even—" And he turned his bleary eyes back towards the hall, where expressions of enthusiasm could be heard emanating from the writers' congress.

"Not even what?" asked the lieutenant.

"Not a thing," said Kopanec. "Not a goddamn thing, comrade lieutenant."

. . .

That same evening, the lieutenant went to the Odeon bar. Many years of experience had honed the barman's memory. With great assurance he confirmed that Mr. Kopanec had in fact been there. He even remembered precisely what he had drunk and how much. It had been a lot. He also recollected that all this had been on Sunday evening. On Saturday, the writer hadn't shown up in the bar at all.

The old detective succumbed to his habitual melancholy and ordered a Becherovka liqueur. Gloomily he looked around the darkened room, which was lined with beige stucco reliefs shaped to represent buxom mermaids. As he was staring at their improbably firm charms, something interrupted him. A beautiful young woman with bright titian hair walked into the bar, accompanied by an elegantly dressed blond man. When she sat down on a stool beside him, the lieutenant noticed that although she was attractive she was not exactly young. He also realized that he knew her. At that moment she recognized him.

"Well, how about that! Lieutenant Boruvka! Hey, I see you're letting your hair down," she said in a friendly voice. "Well, do you remember me or don't you? Olina Zdarska."

"Of course," lied the lieutenant. He remembered the titian hair but not the name. "How are you?"

"I have my good days and my bad days—just like you, I bet. I'm still dancing at the Odeon. This here's Fero Lansky." Having introduced the blond man, she then paid no more attention to him except to order him to order her a whiskey. A Scotch. "I saw you at the funeral this morning. It was real nice of you to come. I mean it. Like, it must be—what?—a couple of years, anyway, since we last had anything to do with you. You haven't been around the theater since then."

"Well, no, I don't suppose you have," said the detective. "I'm investigating the mur—the suicide of Miss Peskova."

"So that's it. Still, it's nice of you. The poor thing." That woman sighed and, using the official—and perhaps even sincere—gloom as an excuse, took a sip of her drink.

"Do you have any idea why she did it?" the lieutenant asked.

"Any idea? I might have. But it's *only* an idea."

"That's enough. Unfortunately it's not a crime."

"Wait a minute! What's not a crime? I thought everything was these days."

"What I meant was that if someone takes his own life because of someone else, that someone else can't be prosecuted for it."

"Ah, then 'unfortunately' is the right word. Because I'd lock the bastard up right now if I could. His only talent is making people suffer."

"Who's only talent?" asked the lieutenant, expecting to hear a name that, so far, had only been connected with literary scandals.

"Ivan Vavra's, of course. That son-of-a-bitch! He never even came to the funeral. As a matter of fact," she said thoughtfully, "that was probably why. Maybe his conscience has finally got to him!"

· · ·

"I'd stay well away from that one, Josef," said Sergeant Malek emphatically. "All you really have to know is that Vavra's got a job with Semtexport. And I don't think we want to know what Semtexport exports. Do you get me?"

The lieutenant had a faint understanding of what Malek was talking about. They didn't write about such things in the Party daily which he glanced through every morning. But he vaguely recalled a rumor of an affair in which a Czechoslovak merchant ship was detained by some foreign customs department because its cargo was not PRAGUE HAM, as was printed across the crates, but something decidedly inedible. He stopped trying to remember the details and said, "I'm not interested in what Semtexport deals in. I'm interested in whether any of their employees travel abroad."

"You're goddamn right they travel abroad! I mean, they export, don't they?"

"What I want to know is whether they import as well," said the lieutenant. "Privately. LSD, for example, or other commodities like that."

"I'd stay clear of that one too!" Malek seemed quite dismayed.

"Why? It's a criminal offense no matter who does it, isn't it?"

"Hey, Josef!" Malek leaned over the table to his superior officer and whispered, "Come on, Josef, you weren't born yesterday. Don't you know who Vavra's boss in Semtexport is? The Old Man's son himself!" And Malek lifted his frightened eyes to the official photograph that hung on the wall: a photograph of the silver-haired president, with thin lips, narrow, steely eyes, and the Order of Lenin on his lapel.

. . .

Despite this most emphatic of warnings, a short time later the lieutenant was stepping out of a trolley bus on Hrebenky. Perhaps it was a result of Malek's warning, but he had a strange sensation. He felt as though he were stepping beyond the borders of one world, his own, and entering another—a world where he would be even more a fish out of water than he was in this world of beautiful young women.

The villa was built in the opulent English country-house style of the 1920s and had probably once belonged to a wealthy industrialist. A young man in a light summer jacket opened the door and led him up a staircase of dark wood to the second floor, where they sat down in an office that was paneled with the same dark wood. Pictures of hunting scenes hung on the walls. The sun entered through a window made up of tiny panels of glass joined by strips of lead. The lieutenant felt as though he were inside a box of expensive cigars. He was overcome by a sudden shyness and stammered out the first few questions—forgetting to look into the face of Ivan Vavra, whose alibi he had come to determine, with his usual acute attention.

The young man admitted, with no sense of embarrassment, that he and the dead dancer had been friends. But, he said, it hadn't been anything serious. The lieutenant wasn't sure what he meant by that, but he did recall that in the girl's correspondence there had been no letters from this elegantly dressed young man. He looked at Vavra's hand. It was holding an American cigarette, and sported a ring with a blue stone. Love letters probably seemed to him just as antiquated as mustache cups or as—the lieutenant searched for a comparison while far below them, outside the window, the city of Prague lay gilded in the evening light—as *conscience*. The comparison had emerged unbidden from the depths of his mind, and it surprised and terrified him. He could not remember where he had got it from. The young man was saying something but now the perspiring writer appeared in his shirtsleeves in the lieutenant's inner vision, reading something the lieutenant could not agree with, while behind him loomed the fat face of the Party secretary. Then he remembered. Yes, that had been the theme of another lecture in politics the Party secretary had once given to the Homicide Division. At the time, the lieutenant had felt the secretary was confusing them with members of the other police. He had spoken about how remnants of bourgeois mentality could hinder the work of the security forces, especially a remnant called Conscience. What the secretary hadn't seemed to realize was that in the Homicide Division's work this remnant still proved useful, and that in some cases they relied on it more than on the deductive capacities of the officers. Moreover, the secretary had spoken about the principle that whatever was good for the Party was correct, regardless of who or what might be harmed; but the lieutenant was not a member of the Party, and the bourgeois remnant called Conscience always reminded *him* of the quiet voice of an insignificant parish priest who had once talked about a similar matter at the Kostelec high school. About ends that justified means. The priest, however, had quoted not from the works of Marx but from the writings of some saint. He had stressed that rather than resort to such means, one should examine one's conscience to see whether it might not be possible to achieve the same ends with other means, means that would not require any justification. The Party secretary was clearly free of such bourgeois prejudices, and went on to speak about having to break eggs to make omelets and about people not being angels. The priest had said this too, but at the same time he had demanded of the lieutenant—then a high-school student—a standard of behavior that only an angel could have lived up to. Nevertheless, the lieutenant had tried.

Unsuccessfully, of course—

"—anything else?"

"What was that? Ah, yes. So you spend all of Saturday night at your cottage with—what was the young lady's name?"

The man butted out his cigarette in an ashtray made of something that looked like glass and had coins embedded in it. The lieutenant could not imagine how this was done. A smile flashed across the young man's face—not of contempt, but rather of amusement. He offered the lieutenant a cigarette, but the old detective shook his head and mechanically pulled out a Virginia-style cigar. The young man held out a mother-of-pearl lighter. Suddenly the high-school student in the lieutenant fell asleep, and the detective was aroused. He began to feel at home in the mahogany-paneled room. Not as a place to live, but as somewhere he could practice his profession.

"Her name is Marie Mouchova."

The lieutenant knew the name. Nevertheless he asked another question, although he knew that answer as well.

"What does she do?"

The young man smiled again. "To tell you the truth, we never discussed her profession."

"Do you have her telephone number?"

"I don't suppose you'll find her at home just now," said the man with the blue ring, and the detective knew that very well too. "Maybe if you tried the Jalta Hotel. . . ."

. . .

The lieutenant felt far more at home in the hotel. It was not the first time he'd been here, and—like this one—all his previous visits had been in the line of duty. In the large restaurant, which was rather full at this time of day, he saw the girl he knew. His acquaintance with her was also in the line of duty: she had once appeared as a witness in a case in which a colleague of hers had been murdered by a waiter who was jealous of a black purchasing agent from the Ghanaian Inland Railway. The girl's name was Marie Mouchova, but at work she used the name Marilyn Mucha.

The lieutenant sat down beside her. She was not pleased, but she knew who the man with the round face was—and knew better than to display any unwillingness to talk to him. So they talked.

"Yes, just me and Ivan," she said with a blank stare.

Although the lieutenant knew women of her profession only in the line of duty, he knew that when they were hired by young men from inconspicuous but important export companies who possessed country houses within easy range from Prague, the purpose was rarely an intimate tête-à-tête.

"Just the two of you, eh?"

"Yes," maintained the girl, and looked at him without affection. "What's so strange about that?"

"It's supposed to be—" the lieutenant searched for the right word "—more fun when there are more people."

He could now see a shadow of mockery in the girl's eyes. "What d'you know about such things?"

He felt his face turning red, so he said in his cold, line-of-duty voice, "More than you would believe, Miss Mouchova. Not from participating in that sort of—frolicking." He stared at her with eyes that were now also very much on duty. "Strictly from records of criminal investigations."

At the trial of the waiter who had put sexual passion ahead of selling foreign currency at a profit, Marilyn had offered testimony which, although not entirely false, hadn't been as straight as a plumb line either. Now it seemed to the detective that she paled a little. But she immediately regained control of herself.

"Oh my!" she exclaimed. "Am I mixed up in something without knowing it again?"

The gloomy detective got up and said, "You can relax, Miss Mouchova. Prostitution isn't my beat. I'm investigating a murder."

And he walked out, leaving Marilyn Mucha in a state of unpleasant uncertainty—which was exactly what he intended.

. . .

It was the summer holiday season, when people left Prague to spend time in the country, but the detective's hopes that he might learn something about that Saturday evening from Ivan Vavra's neighbors came to nothing. Vavra's cottage had no neighbors. It stood alone at the edge of a wood on a hillside overlooking a distant village of white and beige farmhouses. Above the village, like a big, bright ruby, shone the freshly repaired onion tower of a little baroque church. From the wood behind the cottage, a green meadow sloped down to a road that disappeared into another wood. The approach to the cottage was from behind, along a private road that had obviously been constructed at the same time as the cottage. It had certainly not been built by Ivan Vavra—the cottage must have been at least as old as he was, and the lieutenant tried gloomily to estimate what it was worth.

He had had some experience in that. Mrs. Boruvka longed for a cottage of her own, and from time to time the detective was compelled to ask around. But all such recreational facilities cost far more than he could afford; he had no property, and although his pay was enough to support a family of four, in all his years with Homicide he had managed to save only thirty-five thousand crowns. He had spent the entire amount on a family sports coupé that had immediately preceded the cottage on Mrs. Boruvka's scale of desires, and ever since he had bought the car all his extra money had gone to paying off the loan of the ten thousand crowns he had needed to complete the purchase of the car when his wife's longing for it had finally become unbearable. Now Mrs. Boruvka needed only a cottage to be completely happy. They had a flat in Mala Strana; they had sublet a room there as newlyweds and eight years later, when the landlady died, they had officially taken the flat over, after the lieutenant gave a rather thick sealed envelope to one of the comrades in the housing department. They owned a combination phonograph and radio, and a television set. They also owned a refrigerator, for which the lieutenant had stood in line all night in front of the White Swan Department Store. And they had the sports coupé. The lieutenant reckoned he wouldn't be able to buy a cottage for another five years, and then only with another loan. What Mrs. Boruvka would want after that, he had no idea.

Perhaps a new car, he sighed, staring at the cottage. In any case, he'd never be able to afford a place like this. It was a large building in the alpine style, with a wide veranda, a high, peaked gable, and decorative stones on the roof. It must have cost—what, seventy thousand? Eighty thousand? He had never even enquired about a cottage like this.

He walked around the white and green building and peered in through the windows. In one room there was a huge fireplace, and armchairs upholstered in dappled leather. The other room was a kitchen with a propane stove with a portable gas tank, and a large sideboard stacked with dishes. In the room with the fireplace there was a bar with bottles on it. At the back of the cottage there was a private telephone line; it was strung up on low poles along the approach road, and disappeared somewhere into the woods.

The lieutenant was hot and hungry. He thought of Malek. That morning he'd asked him to ask around the bars to see if he could find out where the drunken writer had been on Saturday evening. Not that he really needed the information, but he suspected that Malek would be reluctant to come with him to a cottage belonging to a Semtexport employee, and he didn't like putting his co-workers in embarrassing situations.

. . .

He looked around. It was summertime. The wood was redolent of the unreal smells of a world that was so far only marginally touched by the civilization of sports coupés—the aroma of wild strawberries, raspberries, blackberries, the musk of mushrooms and blueberries. The lieutenant wasn't even sure what was in season at that time of year, but he was hungry, so he waded into the bushes behind the cottage and set off into the woods in search of some of those wild fruits of nature.

There—without realizing just how important it was—he discovered something that made him swear like a heathen. Though the forest seemed virtually untouched by the culture of motorcars, city dwellers had nevertheless left their mark there. The lieutenant had stepped right into a small heap of human excrement.

He cursed and backed out of the bushes into the meadow, where he spent some time carefully wiping off his soiled shoe in the high green grass. At the same time he noticed that a patch of grass had quite recently been used by some rather undisciplined hikers: around the remains of a small campfire were strewn several empty beer bottles, two tin cans that had once held corned beef, and a lot of cigarette butts. He looked at the mess in disgust and then stepped back into the woods to look for strawberries.

Suddenly he stopped, turned around and retraced his steps to the remains of the campfire. He turned over one of the tin cans with the toe of his shoe and then picked up a crumpled newspaper. He smoothed it out; it was last Saturday's paper. He looked around. A short distance from the fire he found a rectangle of flattened grass, partially recovered, where someone had obviously pitched a tent. There was even a forgotten tentpeg sticking out of the grass, and a short distance away there were three used rubber items that had been carelessly discarded—devices the lieutenant had sometimes asked for in drugstores in his youth, but always in a muted voice and then only when he'd found a male sales clerk.

He stood perplexed over these remnants. Years ago he had spent such nights himself, and had always resorted to the confessional afterwards. Today, now that he was past fifty, what scandalized him most were the beer bottles and the tin cans. Back when he had been young and sinful in the woods around Kostelec, he had always dug little holes and buried the sausage wrappers and soda-water bottles—and even those used rubber devices. He had never been able to stand littering.

Ironically, in his present profession the litter was more useful to him than respect for Forest Administration regulations would have been. He walked briskly into the woods, broke a branch from a tree, stripped the leaves and twigs off it, and then went back into the bushes to where he had committed the sin of profanity a short while before. The disgusting thing was lying there covered with buzzing flies, and a piece of paper was sticking out of it. It was not newspaper, much less a tissue. Gingerly the lieutenant used the branch to separate it from the heap. His stomach began to heave, but that was a professional hazard and he had learned to control it. When he had more or less managed to straighten the paper out with the branch, he discovered that it was a post office lettergram, and that there was a message on it in uneven letters:

Franta, cough up that hunnerd crons or else.

The rest of the text was blurred and illegible, but the lieutenant didn't care. He turned the paper over with the branch. On the other side, in the same uneven hand, was an address:

Comrade
Fr. Kokorin
Prague

The rest of the address was also illegible. But the lieutenant did not need the address because he knew who "Fr. Kokorin" was.

And then, despite his professional resistance to such things, he felt sick. He tossed the branch aside, plunged through the bushes, ran out to the sundrenched hillside in front of the cottage, and collapsed onto the grass.

· · ·

He lay there for a long time while his stomach and his mind churned. The proud gables of the neighborless cottage shone white and green in the sun. He turned away and looked across the meadow girded by the woods, and beyond it, down into the distant valley, where columns of bright smoke rose from the chimneys of the village. His stomach gradually calmed but he was overcome by a deep sadness. He turned over and inhaled the fresh smell of the meadow. Butterflies were chasing each other around his head and a large capricorn beetle with long feelers was crawling through the grass; the lieutenant watched its pointless, meandering pilgrimage, and his sadness changed into senseless, perhaps unexplainable despair.

And then he noticed something. He reached out and touched it, thought of picking it, but at the very last instant asked himself: why? He tried not to be superstitious. And anyway, it hadn't brought luck to the dead dancer lying on the green couch in those terribly poignant evening clothes.

He stood up and walked back to his car, leaving the four-leaf clover to live out its own brief life.

· · ·

At the time, Frantisek Kokorin had got off with a conditional sentence and had escaped being sent to reform school because he was at an age officially referred to as "post-juvenile." There'd been a fight. What over? No one could remember. They had all been heavily under the influence and it had just happened. One of them had pulled a knife and it had all been over. They hadn't had anything on Kokorin at the time, except that he'd been present. The lieutenant remembered him because the "post-juvenile" had cried during interrogation. Not because he'd been beaten up. But because the hapless murder victim had been his best friend.

From the very beginning of this new interrogation the lieutenant had to work hard to reassure him. No, he wouldn't tell Libuse's family where she'd been, because Libuse had told her parents she was going camping with her girlfriends. And anyway, even if she hadn't told them that, in this day and age surely—The youngster who had left such a mess in the woods on Saturday finally understood that the lieutenant was not interested in the kind of behavior that Libuse's parents might find objectionable, but purely and simply in whether or not there had been anyone in Vavra's cottage that evening.

"They were having some kind of blow-out in there," the youngster said. "Playing music, making a racket."

"Did you see them?"

"No, just heard them."

How many would you say there were?"

"Hard to say. They were making more noise than a pub full of drunks. And there were two cars outside."

"Did you happen to notice the license numbers, or what kind of cars they were?"

"One was a Tatra 603. Don't know what the other was. A big one. A Renault, maybe—the new kind. But I couldn't say for sure. Oh, wait a minute!" Kokorin swallowed eagerly; he was anxious to help the detective who had once been kind to him. "Yeah, later in the night a Volga arrived. But it left pretty soon afterwards."

"And the other two cars? Did they stay?"

Kokorin shrugged. "We went—you know—to bed. I might have heard the cars start sometime in the night. Anyway, by morning—like about eleven o'clock—they were both gone."

"Thanks," said the lieutenant. "But there's one thing I don't like about this. If you and your girlfriend want to go camping—"

"I'm going to marry her, comrade lieutenant, honest!"

"That's not what I mean," said the detective awkwardly. "But if you must make a mess, then at least don't leave it lying around the woods." He stopped, realizing that such advice was untactical of him, but he decided to finish anyway. "Just take an army shovel with you and bury all your garbage—the tin cans, the bottles, the paper, and the—all the rest of it."

"Hey, you know, I never thought of that," said Kokorin, quite sincerely.

. . .

The lieutenant had little trouble tracking down the owner of the Volga. The central switchboard confirmed that on Saturday night someone had placed a long-distance call from the cottage in Pocelice to a number in Prague which belonged to a Dr. Skala. Dr. Skala turned out to be an assistant to the chief doctor at the Sanops Clinic, an exclusive sanatorium for top Party members and other VIPs.

Sergeant Malek was fed up: he'd been able to find three witnesses to vouch for Kopanec's Saturday night odyssey. Two of them were bartenders, one at the Slice of Bread bar, the other at the Two Ostriches. The third was a doorman at a nightclub called the Cascade, where the besotted writer had been demanding a prostitute; the doorman had carried him outside and stuck him in a taxi. That had been at three o'clock in the morning, and the sergeant had not bothered to trace the taxi driver. Regretfully, he considered this alibi sufficiently airtight to thwart all his hopes of making a politically safe arrest.

Then the lieutenant informed the sergeant of the results of his own investigations.

"It smells, Josef, it really smells!" the sergeant complained, as soon as the lieutenant mentioned Sanops. "Maybe we'd better—"

"Maybe we'd better what?"

"I don't know, let the major handle the case. Shouldn't we? I mean, we're dealing with something—"

"What are we dealing with?"

"Josef, for all I know maybe this whole thing falls under—I don't know—the Official Secrets Act or something—"

"But the victim was just an ordinary dancer—"

"But *she's* not the point!" protested Malek.

"But she *is* the point!" said the lieutenant, almost raising his voice. "What do you think we're doing here? What do you think they pay us for? Why have they given us this trust?"

"Oh, I know all that. But I just—" The sergeant scratched his rumpled hair nervously. During more relaxed cases he usually wore his hair flawlessly slicked back. "There's a Tatra 603 mixed up in it, Josef," he whined. "You know they don't sell Tatra 603s to people like you and me. Anyway, I say we put the ball in the major's court—"

Boruvka almost felt sorry for his distressed subordinate. "Well," he said, "if it will make you feel any better, why don't you find out what Kopanec did on Saturday after they put him in the taxi?"

"What the hell could he have done? The taxi driver cleaned him out and—" He stopped, as it dawned on him that his superior officer was offering him a tactful way out. Then he clicked his heels together and said briskly, "Yes, sir!"

After he was gone, the lieutenant drove off to the Sanops Clinic.

· · ·

Given the situation that was unfolding, Dr Skala was too intelligent to try to make something up. In answering the detective's questions, he omitted only those things he was not specifically asked about. For his part, the detective avoided asking him about them to see what the doctor would leave out.

"Ivan called me because his girlfriend had been bending her elbow a little too enthusiastically and he was afraid she had alcohol poisoning."

"Did she have alcohol poisoning?"

"No, she didn't, but she was definitely ill. So I gave her an emetic, and then a sedative, and then I went home."

"Did you know she died later that night?"

Dr. Skala looked astonished. "Just a moment, I think we must be talking about different women."

"I'm taking about Miss Peskova."

"I'm talking about Miss Mouchova. Sorry, but I don't know anyone called Peskova. As for Miss Mouchova, I saw her alive and well last night at the Jalta Hotel."

The lieutenant fell silent. The view from Skala's office was a lot like the view from Ivan Vavra's apartment: both commanded a magnificent panorama of Prague. It was late in the evening, and a pleasure boat garlanded with lanterns was steaming up the Vltava. Lieutenant Boruvka said, "And was Mr. Vavra there with her—in the cottage, I mean—alone?"

Dr. Skala shrugged his shoulders. "As far as I could tell. At least, I didn't see anyone else."

On his way out of the clinic the lieutenant thought about what Dr. Skala had left out because he hadn't been asked about it.

The Tatra 603.

Nor had Dr. Skala told him anything to explain how two people could make the kind of noise characterized by Frantisek Kokorin—whose hearing had no doubt been dulled by rock 'n' roll—as "a pub full of drunks." But the doctor was clever; he hadn't excluded the possibility that other people had been in the cottage.

One of the two admittedly present had been a young woman whose professional specialty was parties. And yet, according to Dr. Skala, she had become quite unprofessionally drunk—so much so that her partner had had to call in a doctor all the way from Prague, in the middle of the night.

Tell it to my grandmother, the lieutenant said to himself.

. . .

Next morning, they suddenly took the old detective off the case and transferred him to a case they were not even sure was murder. Major Kautsky himself, the chief of the Homicide Division, took over the Peskova file. The lieutenant concluded that the terrified Malek had acted on his own. "Pavel," he said, "I didn't give you permission to take this to the major."

"Me? To the major? I haven't even been in to see him, Josef! I spent the whole day running down that jerk of a taxi driver and here's the result. That creep Kopanec is definitely out. It's just like

I told you: he tossed his cookies all over the back seat, and to make up for it he gave the driver everything he had on him. Three hundred crowns! The driver was so grateful he tucked him into bed personally. I'd really like to throw the book at guys like that. They're rolling in dough, and all they can do is talk sedition! Did you see this morning's paper? The writers' congress has come out in support of the Israeli aggressor—"

"So you didn't ask the major to transfer us to another case?" the lieutenant interrupted.

"Word of honor, Josef!"

"Then why did they transfer us?"

The sergeant looked around carefully, blinked, leaned close to the lieutenant, and whispered, "What did I tell you, Josef? When it comes to politics, you'll never learn. This has nothing to do with the dame. It's got to do with, you know—first Semtexport, then a Tatra 603, and now, to top it all off, the Sanops Clinic!"

He stood up and in a normal tone of voice added, "You ought to be glad, Josef. We'll have this new case wrapped up in half a day. Old man Kostrohryz, a retired railway worker—a real miser—goes off to see his sister in Rakovnik and never shows up. But his sister says she never invited him in the first place, like the son and daughter-in-law claim she did. Son has a criminal record, already been inside once—embezzlement. And old man Kostrohryz has twenty thousand in a numbered account and someone cleans it out just after he catches the train to Rakovnik."

"It certainly looks like an easy case," said the lieutenant gloomily. "Why don't you handle it yourself? I don't feel very well. I'm taking the day off."

Malek did not protest. He enjoyed working on easy cases by himself, because he was hoping for a promotion.

.   .   .

But the lieutenant did not take the day off. He left his superiors thinking he'd gone with Malek, and then he went to Hrebenka again, by trolley bus.

When Ivan Vavra opened the door, he seemed startled to see

the detective standing there. In any case, the flame of his luxurious lighter trembled as he lit the lieutenant's Virginia cigar in the paneled room.

"I went out to take a look at that cottage of yours," the detective said. "Nice. Very nice meadow. Did you know you've got four-leaf clover growing out there?"

"That a fact?" said Vavra. He lit himself a cigarette, the flame of his lighter trembling more noticeably than before.

"Miss Peskova, your—shall I say—one-time girlfriend," said the lieutenant. "When we found her on Saturday, she was wearing high-heeled shoes. There was a four-leaf clover stuck to the bottom of one of her heels. Obviously, sometime that evening she'd gone for a walk somewhere. Perhaps in a meadow where four-leaf clover grows."

The young man tried to laugh. "Not in my meadow, she didn't. At least, I don't recall seeing her," he said. "I was there with Marie Mouchova, as I've already told you. I hope you've checked it out."

> I asked myself—"Of all melancholy topics, what, according to the *universal* understanding of mankind, is the *most* melancholy?" Death—was the obvious reply. "And when," I said, "is this most melancholy of topics most poetical?" . . . "When it most closely allies itself to *Beauty:* the death, then, of a beautiful woman is, unquestionably, the most poetical topic in the world. . . ."

The lieutenant didn't understand that. He remembered a photograph of Kvetuse, a pretty blonde girl with a beautiful, long face that had been transformed into a beautiful, long cranium. He leafed through a few pages and read again, shuddering:

> With a shriek I bounded to the table, and grasped the box that lay upon it. But I could not force it open; and, in my tremor, it slipped from my hands, and fell heavily, and burst into pieces; and from it, with a rattling sound, there rolled out some instruments of dental surgery, intermingled with thirty-two small, white, and ivory-looking substances that were scattered to and fro about the floor.

His whole body trembled. The beautiful white skull stared at him through the open window. I'll not encounter anything more terrifying than that, he thought, not after this. He turned a few more pages and read again: ". . . the strange anomaly of life . . . feelings, with me, *had never been* of the heart, and my passions *always were* of the mind"—but he didn't understand that either. Still, it horrified him. How could passion—and emotion—from reason. . . .

"Yes, as a matter of fact. I know you're telling the truth. It's just that I doubt it's the whole truth and nothing but the truth.'"I answered every question you put to me."

"Is there anything you'd like to add?"

Vavra butted out his half-smoked cigarette. "I don't know whether this would interest you or not but—Marie got sick. I called my friend Dr. Skala. He came out, gave her some pills, and then left."

"I see," said the lieutenant gloomily, and in his mind he tried to find a place in the picture for those strange things, connections, relationships, whose existence he had not known of until today. Or perhaps he hadn't wanted to know? Those strange liaisons in a society of the equal, a people's democracy. . . . He'd been taken off a murder case involving an ordinary dancer as soon as Semtex-port, a Tatra 603, and Sanops came into the picture. And they gave the case to—to whom? To Major Kautsky?

"I see," he said again. "There are just a few unexplained circumstances here. Miss Peskova died in her bachelor flat. We haven't been able to determine who she was with that evening, or where. However, the autopsy did show that she was drunk. Perhaps she'd been drinking at home; there was a single glass in the flat that had been drunk from, and a bottle that was almost empty. Yet Miss Peskova was wearing an evening gown, and there was that four-leaf clover on her shoe."

"But Dr. Skala's already told you—" Vavra suddenly stopped, aware that he had let something slip. What else had Dr. Skala passed on, wondered the detective, and to whom? Malek—Boruvka believed him—had kept his mouth shut. Or was it Vavra who had told someone? Or even the third man, the owner of the Tatra 603, unseen and unmentioned so far but, as the lieutenant now knew for sure, present in the cottage on the night of the murder? "That is," he heard Vavra trying to cover his tracks, "I assume you've already asked him about it. I'm sure Dr. Skala confirmed that I was alone at the cottage with Marie."

"To be precise, Dr. Skala confirmed that he saw you and Miss Mouchova at the cottage. But it's a big cottage with several rooms and there's a whole second floor where Dr. Skala didn't go—"

"I understand—you have to use your professional imagination," said the young man with a feeble attempt at irony. "But the fact is that Dr. Skola only saw me and Marie there."

"Then there's the strange fact that although she was alone at home, Miss Peskova was wearing an evening gown. When girls like her get home, they usually change into a housecoat, to save their evening gowns. Clothes like that are pretty expensive."

"You said yourself she was drunk. When I come home under the influence I collapse on the bed like a log. With my clothes on."

"Perhaps you can afford to," persisted the detective. "But before she—" he paused "—collapsed on the sofa she warmed some milk."

It seemed to the lieutenant that the elegantly dressed young man had turned pale.

"And the consequences were tragic," he continued. "The milk boiled over, it put the burner out, and Miss Peskova inhaled the gas."

"That happens."

"Yes, it does. But the odd thing is that Miss Peskova didn't die of gas poisoning. She was killed by a drug called LSD. Combined with alcohol, taken in large amounts, it can—so the doctors say— be lethal."

"But Dr. Skala said nothing—"

"Dr. Skala didn't tell me anything I didn't ask him about. For instance, he didn't mention that besides your own car there was also a Tatra 603 parked in front of your cottage. Now, if it didn't belong to Miss Mouchova—" he looked quizzically at the young man, who was butting out another cigarette "—and I rather suspect it didn't, then there must have been some other people at the cottage as well."

There was a long silence. Then the detective said, "I repeat— Miss Peskova had a four-leaf clover stuck to the heel of her shoe."

Vavra sat in his leather armchair, pale, groping for something to say; then he lit another cigarette and inhaled deeply.

"Let me tell you how I think it was," said the lieutenant sadly. "There were four of you at the party. Maybe more; the party was very noisy, and two big cars can accommodate more than four. But four at least: you, Miss Mouchova, Miss Peskova, and another man. You'd had a few drinks, but it wasn't enough—at least, not for some of you. We know, for instance, that Miss Peskova was addicted to drugs. You, or perhaps this other man, gave her LSD. You could, if you wanted to, get hold of it. You go abroad frequently, where that wouldn't be such a problem. Of course, you're not familiar with the effects of LSD, and suddenly Miss Peskova was taken ill. Probably very ill. She passed out, you got scared and called Dr. Skala. He told you things looked bad. But Miss Peskova was still alive, so you worked out a plan. You drove her back to Prague in the middle of the night. You put milk on the stove, waited till it boiled over, then you cleared out. But the plan was improvised and you overlooked several things. That always happens. I have never known any exceptions to that rule."

The lieutenant stopped. Prague lay outside the window, resplendent.

"Is that everything?" asked Vavra.

"Yes. There's only one thing I don't know. Who the second man was."

Vavra stood up, butted out his cigarette—which was smoked only a quarter of the way down—and spoke in a voice he hadn't used so far, a voice that, unlike his fingers, was not trembling. "There was no second man, and even if there was, I'd advise you not to drag him into this. Otherwise it's all nonsense, and I dare you to try and prove that any of it's true!"

. . .

The next day the lieutenant reported what he had learned to Major Kautsky. Instead of praising him, the major was clearly alarmed. First he rebuked the lieutenant for continuing the investigation on his own after he'd been shifted to the Kostrohryz case. Then he tried to refute his arguments.

"It's all more or less circumstantial evidence, comrade lieutenant. We can't build a case on that, not one that the prosecutor would take."

"We can determine the identity of the second man."

"How do you propose going about that?"

"Kokorin will testify that he saw a Tatra 603 parked by the cottage. Vavra will have to come out with the truth."

"What if Kokorin was making it all up?" said the major, but the old detective merely looked reprovingly into his eyes. "Okay, okay, I know, why would he make up something like that? But—but—"

"We've got a murder here and we've got an illegal drug, comrade major. It's a very serious and ugly affair. If they'd taken her to the hospital in Pribram they might have been able to save her life. But instead—anyway, there has to be an investigation."

"Of course. But I don't know whether it's within our competence. It's definitely going to require consultation. I mean, with LSD and other things—"

"That's true. Dr. Seifert says he's had no experience dealing with those new drugs—"

"What I meant was—consultation with Interior," said Major Kautsky.

The lieutenant felt himself going weak. All his old aversion to being identified with that other police force welled to the surface. But this time there was something else, too—something that had terrified the otherwise cool Malek. He was silent, he no longer tried to press his point. He surrendered the case to the major and, through him, to others—but he did not forget about it. Just as he had never forgotten about that *other* case.

. . .

At the time he had managed to put himself on the wrong side of that *other* police force, and it was they who would never forget about it. It had happened during those days of shame brought upon the old detective by his daughter Zuzana when she announced that the man who had brought her to her blessed state was an idiot and a jerk, something she'd had the misfortune of discovering only after it was too late, but fortunately still in time not to marry him. Shortly afterwards, the lieutenant discovered that she was lying: she was refusing to disclose the father's name, not because he was an idiot, but for a different reason altogether. A reason that had put her in danger.

Lieutenant Boruvka had been sitting in front of the television watching a documentary about ski manufacturing, and in his mind still trying to work out a conundrum: would he ever be able to show his face in Kostelec again, with a grandchild but without a son-in-law? Then Zuzana stepped quietly into the room.

"Father, I have something to tell you. Something awful."

The lieutenant took her announcement coolly. It occurred to him that nothing worse than Zuzana's becoming a single mother could possibly happen to him. Gently he said, "Perhaps it won't be as bad as you think."

"Oh, yes, it will, Father. It's very bad, and I have no idea what to do about it."

"Is there any way I can help?"

"Only by giving me some advice."

"I'm glad you trust me, Zuzana. Well, what's the matter?"

"The matter is," said his swelling daughter, "that there's this spook following me around."

"What do you mean?" Filled with obsessive thoughts of the urgently needed son-in-law, the lieutenant blurted, "Does he want to—marry you?" He was immediately overwhelmed by ambiguous feelings: a member of the *other* police force for a son-in-law?

He had an even greater aversion to secret policemen than to murderers. Murderers didn't sully the reputation of his profession. "No, he doesn't want to marry me," said Zuzana, in a voice that was suddenly as gloomy as her father's became when things got really bad. "He just wants—you can guess what."

A wave of rage hit the lieutenant. "The—! How dare he! The filthy-minded—"

"That's natural with spooks. That's how they make a living," said Zuzana.

"Make a living?" Boruvka was puzzled. Then, suddenly, the truth began to dawn on him. "What exactly is it he wants you for, Zuzana?"

"What else would he want? He wants me to nark for him."

The lieutenant, robbed of a rather unattractive hope of father-in-lawhood, said, "That's easy enough to settle. Just turn him down. He can't force you."

"That's just it. He can," said Zuzana.

Again, the lieutenant was shocked. "Are you—in some kind of trouble?"

Zuzana put her hand on her asymmetrical stomach. "Have you forgotten, Father?"

"But—single mothers are common enough today—what I mean to say is, it's no—nothing to be ashamed of. Those are just—bourgeois pre—"

"Oh, I'm sorry," said Zuzana. "I forgot to tell you one little detail. It's got nothing to do with me being a single mother. The problem is that the father of this little bugger in my belly isn't single."

The lieutenant was so crushed that he forgot to reprimand her for describing his future grandchild so inappropriately. "Zuzana! You've been carrying on with—"

"With a married man. Yes, I was, but the bastard didn't tell me and I was too dumb to figure it out right away. I didn't realize until those cops caught us in the hotel."

"Zuzana! In a hotel!"

"Well, where were we supposed to go? We don't own a cottage, neither does he—"

For a moment the lieutenant stopped listening. When he got a grip on himself again, he understood that the results of the hotel identity checks were routinely passed on to officers of that *other* police force. As a result, a proposition had been made to Zuzana: either have the occasional rendezvous, a purely unromantic, informative rendezvous, with a secret policeman, or else be prepared for her lover's wife to find out about her lover's mistress.

"But Zuzana, why should you care? You told me yourself that you don't want any more to do with him."

"That's true, I don't," said Zuzana awkwardly. "But the guy is such a jerk. He's dumb, but he's still nice. And his wife—Father! If they tell her about me, there's no telling what she'll do. She'll probably cut his balls off!"

"Zuzana!"

"All right, she'll unman him. Anyway, the point is, I feel sorry for the stupid jerk, and I can't bring myself to drag him into this." There were some ways in which Zuzana resembled her father. "And they know it!" she added angrily. "They're playing on my delicate feminine sensitivities, the pigs! And I don't know what to do. Maybe pregnancy is turning me into an old hen. If you can't help me, then I guess I'll have to defect to the West. But I don't know how I'd make it over all those hills in this condition— unless I just lie down and *roll* across the border."

The lieutenant thought for a while and then said, "Why don't they go to him with their—bright ideas?"

Zuzana sank back theatrically into the little armchair and quite genuinely started to weep. The lieutenant was stunned, perhaps more than by the revelation itself. His cheerful, resilient daughter—"Oh, Father!" Zuzana wailed. "Because they already *have* him! He confessed to me. And yet—I still can't do it to him! Oh, Daddy!" His calm daughter, so richly endowed with a sense of humor, succumbed to hysterics. "I don't know what to do-o-o-o!"

· · ·

What came next was one of the most difficult tasks in the lieutenant's entire career. Very delicately he told the wronged wife what had happened and begged for her understanding and forgiveness. He hoped to take the wind out of the other police's sails, and in this, at least, he succeeded.

In the end the wife forgave. But not until the bitter end. Before that happened, of course, the lieutenant was thrown out of the idiot's flat. This was followed by a dramatic confrontation between husband and wife and, after that, one with Zuzana, whom the wife labeled a slut, a whore, and an intellectual. Then the wronged woman took the children (she and the idiot had four), ran home to her mother, and lodged a complaint with the Party cell (the idiot was a Communist). There was a detailed hearing before the Party committee, the Party served the idiot with an official reprimand, and finally there was a comradely reconciliation between husband and wife. Six months later the idiot, obviously not unmanned, got mixed up with another woman and the whole thing had a rerun, only this time the slut, whore, and intellectual was a Party member too. But that was no longer any concern of the lieutenant's.

What did concern him was the fact that the idiot's Party organization had learned about the lieutenant's intervention in the affair. There must have been at least one comrade in that organization, and perhaps two or three, who passed this information on to the appropriate places. The detective was justifiably afraid that in those places they had classified his action as a willful undermining of the interests of the working class.

. . .

A few days after he had personally taken over the Peskova case, Major Kautsky called the lieutenant into his office. He was unusually mild-mannered and offered the lieutenant a glass of vodka. To be polite (and because he liked vodka) the lieutenant accepted. In the course of the conversation he let the major refill his glass many times, and sometimes he even refilled it himself.

"Comrade lieutenant," the major began, "I'm going to talk to you not as your superior officer but as your friend. Murder is a terrible thing. A crime. There can be no debate about that. Under normal circumstances it must be harshly but justly punished. But here—" The major looked out the window. Part of the façade of St. Sidonius was visible. From his window the lieutenant could see the whole church, including the plaster saint that was permanently soiled by a pair of pigeons who had thrown a nest together directly above the saint's head. "Here," the major went on, "it seems there are—how shall I put this—interests, shall we say, that have a wider import—"

He noticed that the lieutenant had finished his vodka and he quickly poured him another.

"Our society is deeply democratic," he began again, in the kind of voice he used during political meetings in the Homicide squad. "On the other hand, we must not forget that this is a democra' of a new kind. We know," and the lieutenant had the same impression he often had at those meetings, that the major's phraseology did not precisely correspond to the major's private way of thinking, "that democracy is not the same as egalitarianism. We also know that the guarantee of this democracy is the leading role—" and the lieutenant stopped listening as his thoughts drifted away. He was no longer sitting in the Homicide Division but in the hall where the Party secretary sat and where a perspiring writer was reading from a prepared speech. Because he hadn't eaten since morning, the vodka made him feel as though he were floating around in an unreal haze. He waved his empty glass and the major, without interrupting his lecture, tipped the bottle and poured him another drink. "Anything that harms the Party, anything that tarnishes its good name, is essentially anti-democratic, and subjective intentions are irrelevant. Even if those intentions were pure as the driven snow, objectively—" and the lieutenant's attention, focused on the vodka, drifted off once again, and from a distance he heard the major's voice, "we cannot measure them by the same standards as we do other citizens, even though of course they are completely equal otherwise. However they represent not only themselves as people, but also . . ." *not one human problem was solved*—"that would be egalitarianism," said the major, and he added unhappily, "False egalitarianism, because—"

Something old in the lieutenant rebelled.

"But comrade major! This is murder! Premeditated murder! If it had been done in a fit of passion—but they—well, it was in cold blood. I don't know, maybe this egalitari—agilatri—" He couldn't get the word out and he wilted. He held out his glass; the major readily filled it, hesitated, then filled his own glass as well. Suddenly he changed his phraseology and said, "I know, Josef—you don't mind if I call you Josef, do you?"

Confused, overwhelmed by a sense of insufficient knowledge of the world, the lieutenant said, "Go right ahead."

"They're a bunch of skunks, Josef. Spoiled brats. They think they can get away with everything. And it's not the first time— though it's never been this serious before, but—And don't worry, they won't get away with it so easily this time. They'll send them to some asshole of the world, to Tanzania or Angola or some place like that," said the major, who was usually very proper. He tossed back his glass and poured himself another one. "But—hand it over to the public prosecutor? He'll never allow that." He looked up to the face on the wall, with its thin lips and silvery hair, then unhappily at his subordinate, noticed the state of his glass, and corrected it. "What else can I tell you, Josef?"

A merry-go-round was spinning out of control inside the lieutenant's head, driven by vodka, by that voice, by that old story— but he managed to stammer weakly, "But don't you remember, Ed, we once took an oath." He felt some of his former pluck returning. "I can understand it—certain privileges—they have it tough up there—not like us. But the girl is what this is all about. She was foolish, miserable, unhappy, and she'd been through this disgusting business once before, do you remember? With that scoundrel of a prosecutor—Hynais?"

The major nodded.

"I'm sorry, Ed," stammered the lieutenant. "I can't—I have

to—" An involuntary sigh tore itself loose from the major's chest. He poured himself another glass, drank it, and then filled the lieutenant's glass.

"Look, Josef," he said in a tired voice. "Please, believe me. I have nothing to do with this. But *they,*" and he stressed the ominous, vague, and yet so concrete pronoun, "—*they* told me that— if you won't see reason, they've got things they can pull out—"

"They've got nothing on me!" said the drunken lieutenant defiantly. The major looked at him. It was a long, sad look full of regret.

"I—I've always strictly observed the law!" said the lieutenant with much less defiance.

"The laws aren't the only things you can trip up on, Josef," said the major, taking the telephone off the hook. "There was a—a comrade here to see me. Now, I want you to understand, I don't hold it against you, not in the least. I understand it, believe me, I do. But apparently you've been—carrying on or something, I don't know how to put it, with a certain singer—"

A wave of cold fear washed over Lieutenant Boruvka. He held out his glass. The major filled it up.

"You've got a family, Josef. Your daughter's going to the university. You've got a boy who's about to graduate from high school. Think about them. You can't help that poor girl now. And I tell you again, those bastards are going to be cooling their asses far away from here in some godforsaken place. But you're a good man, so why should you—and your family—suffer, and for no good reason whatever?"

The lieutenant took a drink. He felt tiny as an ant, lost in a terrifyingly inegalitarian democratic society. . . . *Citizen,* he heard the sweaty author, *that was once a glorious, revolutionary word.* . . . He saw Zuzana expelled from school, seduced and abandoned; he saw his son, Joey, as a bricklayer's apprentice somewhere, if he was lucky; he saw his good-natured, tearful wife, whom he had shamefully betrayed with the blonde globetrotter. . . .

He held out his glass. The major turned the bottle upside down.

The case of Alena Peskova entered the records as suicide by asphyxiation.

. . .

"Just like I told you, Josef." Sergeant Malek was glowing. "I had him behind bars in half an hour. I tell you, the place stank like a pile of Limburger cheese under glass. God, they were stupid. They bricked old man Kostrohryz up in the wall—a real amateur job—in the corner of the kitchen, so by the time we got through to him we just about had to mop him up off the floor. That's how far gone he was. Where are you going, Josef?"

The lieutenant didn't say a word. Perhaps his stomach had turned at the sergeant's humor.

"They're going to hang. Both of them," declared Malek. "Not only was it cold-blooded premeditation, but they had supper there every day in the stench from their own father!"

The old detective closed the door quietly behind himself and walked away.

. . .

That evening he sat in the darkened room in his easy chair. The television was dead. Next door Zuzana and Mack were playing records. It had developed into one of those cases he was familiar with from his work: Mack had fallen in love with his daughter when she was in her ninth month. And he wasn't even put off by the prospect of a purely honorary paternity, even though he was an American. Or perhaps precisely because he was an American. The lieutenant had heard somewhere that Americans tended to be oversentimental in love.

He smiled and felt his sorrow lifting a little. Perhaps he had done the right thing. God knew what else they could have done to his daughter, to his—but still it kept eating away at him, and it spoiled his delight in seeing a nice young couple who might have a nice future together. . . . What was it? The same thing he had heard condemned in the Party secretary's political lectures? That old prejudice, that old relic? Something that, long ago, the venerable Father Meloun—

Next door they put on the familiar tune again. He listened to the slow, syncopated rhythms.

> And the moment before she died . . .

He listened, drinking in the sounds of the saxophones.

> She lifted up her lovely head and cried . . .

He stood up and walked over to the window. In the distance, beyond the roofs of the city, there was an empty bachelor flat where a none-too-proper, rather unhappy, pretty, lonely, and insignificant nightclub dancer had lost her life. By now there must be a lot of people interested in her flat. . . .

> Miss Otis regrets . . .

Miss Otis? Who was Miss Otis? Miss Peskova. Miss Alena Peskova regrets.

The lieutenant hung his head. Even Zuzana, secure now with her apparently faithful Mack, could not make him happy. Not even the music could help him.

Strange Archaeology

It had been Boruvka's first case. Back then he wasn't allowed to deal with homicides, only missing persons, and someone called Kvetuse Rerichova had disappeared. She was a clerk with the State Savings Bank on Wenceslas Square.

. . .

He looked around the little room she shared with her mother. Against one wall stood two narrow couches made of old packing crates. They were painted red and doubled as beds at night. The room itself was narrow with a window at one end that looked out on a litter-strewn courtyard with open-air walkways running around its perimeter. Swinging in the breeze on clotheslines strung across the yard were brassieres, long underwear, and delicate blouses with flower and polka-dot patterns. The room also contained a modest bookshelf constructed from orange crates. It held volumes of poetry, and a cheap Bakelite record player rested on top of it. There was a man's shaving mirror on a small table between the couches. Since the girl's mother slept on the second couch, and her ten-year-old brother, whose bed was in the kitchen, was the only male in the household, the mirror obviously served as a vanity table. It made you seem bigger when you looked into it.

"They moved us in here when Dad and Ota fled the country, commissioner," said the old lady tearfully. She was wearing a threadbare housecoat and her hair looked like what Boruvka's former boss, Lieutenant Soukup, called "piss-soaked straw." "We used to have a three-room flat for the seven of us. Now there's only four of us and all we got is this room and the kitchen, but there's no window in the kitchen."

"Four?" asked Boruvka, who was still a sergeant at the time. "How's that? There's you, your daughter, your son—?"

"Ruda—well, he tried to escape with Dad and Ota, but they caught him. He's still doing time."

"Oh, I see," said Boruvka. His eyes wandered to the wall, where among magazine reproductions of van Gogh's golden yellow sunflowers hung a photograph of two men, one younger, one older, leaning nonchalantly against a large American car. A sign on a store in the background read BEN'S BURGER BURG. Sergeant Boruvka had no idea what that meant, but he could guess where the picture had been taken. The woman saw what he was looking at.

"Well, that's where they are—New York," said the woman. "Dad—my husband—writes that he's the manager of some company that rents apartment buildings. Only in America, he says, he's called a 'superintendent.' But he doesn't manage to send us much money. If it weren't for Kvetuse, I don't know what we'd. . . . I can't get work anywhere because of my husband. Libuse's moved out and lives on her own, but Kvetuse's a good girl. She hands over all her wages to me except for a little spending money she keeps back for herself." The woman with the straw-colored hair began to cry.

"That's all right, ma'am," said Boruvka. "We'll have the matter cleared up in no time. Now, tell me what happened. I understand your daughter told you she was just going away for the day with her boyfriend on Sunday. Is that what she said?"

"That's right, commissioner. She packed a suitcase—and I—"

"You what?"

"Officer! After she went, I looked, and she'd taken everything she owned with her!"

"What do you mean, everything?"

"Well, she took the business suit I altered for her when Libuse left, both her dresses, all her underthings, two rings and a necklace she got from her grandmother, and both pairs of shoes. And she said she was only going away for the day—"

Sergeant Boruvka frowned. Once again, he looked at the photograph of the two smiling men beside the shiny big car. The case began to appear very straightforward.

"What did she leave behind?"

"Nothing but this record player and a couple of books. She even took her favorite books with her." The woman looked at the constable in alarm. "Maybe I shouldn't even have reported it."

An inexplicable sadness came over Boruvka, but he managed to put on a severe expression. "It was your responsibility and you did the right thing. But"—he hesitated—"I don't think you have anything to worry about." He looked at his assistant—the old chief constable, Sintak, whom they allowed to remain on the force only because he had agreed to leave the Church, although Boruvka was aware that each Sunday he drove all the way to Kremosin, where no one knew him, to attend mass. From Sintak's expression, Boruvka could see that what he was about to say would remain confidential. He smiled at the weeping woman. "To tell you the truth, ma'am, it probably won't be long before you'll be hanging a picture of your daughter beside the other two, in front of that"—he leaned closer to the photograph—"BEN'S BURGER BURG, whatever that is."

"I pray to God you're right, sir."

"I'm afraid I am," said the sergeant. Then he resumed his official composure. "Of course, the fact remains that your daughter has done something that is not only very foolish but also against the law." The old lady began to sob so plaintively that the sergeant, after another glance at Sintak, added, "Anyway, let's hope the border guards—" and he stopped.

Sintak broke into a wide grin. "No way, Mr.—I mean comrade sergeant. They'd have nabbed her long before this. She's been gone a week already. Your daughter must be a pretty sharp kid, ma'am."

. . .

Sergeant Boruvka soon had reason to agree that Kvetuse Rerichova was indeed a pretty sharp kid.

"Twenty thousand?" he asked her department head at the State Savings Bank. His voice was incredulous.

"That's right. She withdrew the lot a day before she disappeared."

She gives all her wages to me, except for a little spending money for herself. Hmm, thought the sergeant. This is going to be more complicated than I thought.

"I'm afraid I may have had a hand in it myself," said the department head. He was a youthful, dark-haired man with a Young Communist League button in his lapel. "At the league meeting last week, I proposed that she be fired."

"Why?"

"Loss of confidence. She was a good teller. But as a citizen?" And he began to count on his fingers. "Father a small businessman, arrested for provocative behavior towards a government inspector right after the Revolution in 1948. As soon as he gets out of prison, he escapes to the West with his elder son. Her second brother is caught attempting to cross the border. Her mother is unemployed and has had run-ins with the security forces for making inappropriate political statements. And the money we handle here belongs to our working people. We can't afford to employ comrades who don't enjoy our full confidence."

"Where did the twenty thousand come from?" asked Boruvka.

"I don't know. I had no idea myself she had so much money. She had a password account."

Boruvka frowned. Her account was empty, her suitcases were

packed with all her worldly possessions, her father was in America. Everything pointed to the same simple, unmysterious conclusion. All that was left to explain was where the twenty thousand crowns had come from.

. . .

That didn't remain a mystery for long, either. Looking through the files, Boruvka discovered that the friend with whom Kvetuse was to have gone on the trip had a criminal record: three years for attempting to cross the border and for poor behavior in prison. The girl had been surrounded by criminals and the circumstances of her disappearance were becoming clearer all the time. Except the money.

"She won it in the lottery," explained the friend, Miroslav Jun. "She bet half her spending money each week, and this February she hit the jackpot."

Jun had nervous eyes, but he was a handsome young man. Despite his criminal record, the sergeant felt he could trust him. The wastepaper depot where he was questioning him was a dark room with a large weigh-scale in the middle and stacks of old newspapers piled up along the walls. A long line of aged women stretched out the door; each woman carried a bundle of old newspapers in a shopping bag, obviously gathered from garbage cans and tied with bits of knotted string. An elderly man in a pair of ragged overalls stood by the scales. He weighed the bundles, then handed each old lady some coins.

"So you didn't go out with her on Saturday?"

"No."

"Where were you?"

"At home. I'm learning . . . English. I studied all weekend."

"Can anyone vouch for you?"

The young man said nothing but shook his head. "No. My landlady went to see her son in Benesov."

"Do you know why I'm asking you these questions?" Boruvka's eyes met the young man's. They were guarded but bold. "No," replied the young man rebelliously.

"She's missing, her money's gone from her bank account, her suitcase—"

"So how come I'm still here?" His voice was now arrogant, with a trace of sarcasm in it.

"Maybe you figured it wasn't worth risking it a second time."

"That's God's own truth," said the young man with feeling. "But what's Kvetuse's taking off got to do with me?"

"We don't know if she actually has—taken off, as you put it."

"So what do you want of me?"

For a moment, Sergeant Boruvka merely looked into the young man's nervous eyes. Then, thoughtfully, he replied, "In an abandoned quarry near Karlovy Vary we found the bodies of seven girls. It was always the same story: bank accounts cleared out, suitcases packed. The first one disappeared two years ago. The last one nine months ago."

The young man grinned. "I was still behind bars, in case you've forgotten."

"I hadn't forgotten. And we've got the scoundrel. He promised to take those poor girls across the border. They all ended up in the quarry."

"I don't see what that's got to do with—" the young man began, then stopped. "Oh, you think—"

The sergeant nodded. Then he said, "Those girls in the quarry aren't the only cases like that, just the ugliest."

The young man's insolence suddenly vanished. In a trembling voice, he said, "But I was fond of Kvetuse. I'd never have—for a lousy twenty thousand. And anyway, I tried to per—" He stopped suddenly.

"What did you try to persuade her?" Boruvka said encouragingly.

Jun saw at once that he had said something he couldn't take back. He looked at Boruvka and then at Sintak. The sergeant's round face was not like the faces he'd been used to seeing in the past three years. Even Chief Constable Sintak seemed more human than the goons in prison. In his irrepressibly good natured way,

Sintak said, "Come on, out with it. Don't be afraid, we're not going to—" and he glanced at the sergeant, who pretended he hadn't heard.

The young man was intelligent and his instincts were sound. "Kvetuse did want to skip the country," he said, "that's a fact. And I didn't report her to the police, that's also a fact."

"But you tried to persuade her not to go," said Sintak. "In my book that's an ex—an ex—what is it the lawyers say? Anyway, it lets you off the hook."

"It's an extenuating circumstance, that's true," interrupted the sergeant. "Tell us what happened."

"I told her not to be crazy, but she wouldn't listen. You know, her dad and her brother are already living in the United States; she told me her brother was doing well selling cars, and she was fed up to the teeth with that hole she was living in. She had nothing to wear, either. Once we were out on a date—" and he stopped. "But that has nothing to do with this case."

"Go ahead, tell us," coaxed Boruvka.

"Well—it was last January. Before she won the lottery. It was freezing cold but a nice, sunny day. She showed up in a purple corduroy jacket and we went for a walk on Petrin Hill. She wasn't saying much that day, and I was blabbing on—you know, about books, because she loved reading and talking about them—and suddenly it seemed strange how quiet she was, like a wooden statue, so I look and she's all blue, shaking like a leaf. The thing was, not only did she not have a winter coat, she didn't even have a sweater on underneath. She had no money. So I took her into a pub and poured at least five mulled wines into her before she got her voice back. Then I bought her a sweater. I'm only telling you that, sir," the young man went on, "so you'll know how hard up they were, so you'll understand that she had good reason—even though it doesn't excuse her, naturally."

"Well—" Sintak began, but the sergeant quickly interrupted him.

"You tried to dissuade her, but she—"

"She wanted me to put her in touch with someone who would

take her across, but I didn't know anybody. If I did, I wouldn't be working in this scrap-paper depot today. And then she—" Once more he fell silent.

"She what?"

"Well—-she still wanted to clear out. She was obsessed with the idea."

The sergeant sighed. "Look, Mr. Jun. You didn't report an intent to commit a crime, and now you're holding something back from us again. As for not reporting her—well, there *are* extenuating circumstances, I agree. But they'll only be extenuating if you tell us *everything* you know, not just *some* things."

One of the old ladies in the line began to cough uncontrollably. The man in the overalls took the bag out of her hand and removed a pile of newspapers. They were of prewar vintage and the paper was brittle and yellowed. The woman had obviously found them stashed away in someone's attic.

"Where did you get these, ma'am?"

The old lady tried to reply but she was still coughing too violently to speak.

"Sit down here, ma'am," said the man in the coveralls, indicating the scales. He began leafing through the old papers with great interest. "I'll buy these from you myself. There's a lot of good reading here, ma'am." He looked at the scales. "That's thirty-eight kilos, which makes—" and he pulled a wallet out of his back pocket. It was well worn, but made of snakeskin, and he extracted two banknotes from it.

Boruvka was fascinated by the scene. This man can't have spent all his life weighing scrap paper, he thought. For a moment he forgot the investigation, but the young man himself brought the sergeant back to the subject.

"All right, I'll tell you," he said dejectedly. "She was at my place the day before she disappeared. She came to say goodbye. And she said she'd found a way herself. I thought it was better not to ask for any details. I tried to persuade her not to go again, but her mind was made up."

"Hmm," said the detective, looking the young man in the eye. For the first time, he saw the flash of contempt that would, later in his career, become a familiar sight. For the first time, too, he felt defensive about his job. The young man's expression made him feel ashamed and sad. The story of the shivering young girl had moved him. Even since his youth, Boruvka had been more than ordinarily sentimental. "Hmm," he said again. For the young man's sake, he came up with a ridiculous conclusion. "You thought she was just paying you back for your unwillingness to help her. You didn't really believe her but you let her think you did because you were fond of her. Isn't that how it was?"

The contempt disappeared from the young man's eyes and was replaced by something else. Boruvka was glad to see that his name would not be consigned to that certain category.

"Yes, sergeant. I knew all along she was just kidding."

. . .

And thus the case of Kvetuse Rerichova, a teller in the State Savings Bank, was closed. An illegal crossing of the border, successfully completed. It was a common occurrence at the time. Boruvka was praised for his quick work, and very shortly afterwards he was assigned to his first murder case, which he solved with equal swiftness. For a while, he gave serious thought to requesting a transfer to Petty Theft. The case had involved a perverted driver's mate who had murdered his wife, packed her in ice, and kept her in the basement for two months while having sexual intercourse repeatedly with the corpse. For a month afterwards, Boruvka had nightmares and woke up soaked in his own sweat, wondering whether it was all worth it. At last, thinking the worst was now behind him, he decided to remain with the Homicide Division.

. . .

Eleven years had gone by since the disappearance of Kvetuse Rerichova. By this time, the sergeant—now a lieutenant (he would never be promoted beyond that because he remained reluctant to join the Communist Party, on the grounds that his consciousness had not yet been sufficiently raised)—had a reputation which, in criminological circles, extended beyond the borders of the state. He had even been invited to give a paper to an international criminological congress in Warsaw. The paper was reprinted (after having been stylistically overhauled by a certain policewoman) in the *Criminological Gazetteer,* along with an abstract in three languages.

One day, the lieutenant was summoned to a new housing development in Krc, on the outskirts of Prague. Some workers digging the foundations for a co-operative apartment block on a piece of land where a small woodlot had once stood had unearthed a human skull.

. . .

The skull, cleaned and beautifully white, stood on Dr. Seifert's laboratory table, gleaming like alabaster in the afternoon sunshine. Dr. Seifert turned it over, revealing an ugly hole in the elegantly elongated cranium.

"A blow from a pointed object," said Dr. Seifert, who enjoyed speaking technically whenever he made professional statements. "That's what killed her." He turned the skull over again and pointed: "A fractured supra-orbital margin, broken nasal bone, both maxillae have sustained blows from a blunt object, the right maxilla has collapsed and bone fragments have lodged in the nasal cavity, teeth quite sound but three have been knocked out. Left temple punctured—"

"A maniac?" asked the lieutenant.

Dr. Seifert slowly shook his head. "I doubt it. It may look that way, but there's one circumstance that gives me pause—"

"You mean the fact that he separated the head from the body and buried it separately?"

"No, not that. A body without a head is difficult to identify. It's something else."

The doctor placed a finger on the bare, chalk-white crown. "It hasn't been in the ground for more than ten, fifteen years. It's a female cranium. Looking at the teeth, I'd say a girl of about twenty-five. And there's no sign of her hair."

"Maybe it rotted."

"No, no," said Dr. Seifert. "There would still be something left after ten years. The murderer scalped her."

"But why?"

"Perhaps he'd read some true-crime stories," said Dr. Seifert, shifting from his technical style to the language he usually used when dealing with the detective. "Something about Dr. Crippen, perhaps. They nailed Crippen on the basis of an appendix scar on a piece of skin from the stomach of his wife. Our killer simply scalped his victim so we couldn't identify her by the color of her hair." He was silent for a moment, then added, "And I would say he did something even more gruesome. First he tried to deform the face, and then, just to make sure, he boiled the head"—Dr. Seifert stopped and looked at the lieutenant, who had become almost as pale as the skull—"and he disposed of the fleshy parts. Otherwise there's no explanation for why the bone is so clean and white."

The old detective swallowed and stared at the skull. It was narrow and well shaped. The girl must have had a narrow, noble face. It reminded him of something, something he had read recently and put down in disgust—he couldn't remember what.

"He must have cut the rest of the body into pieces, like Crippen," said Dr. Seifert. "I wouldn't be surprised if we heard from other building sites. There's a lot of construction going on these days."

"They found a hand not long ago," said the lieutenant in an unsteady voice. "It was impossible to identify. No fractures, no tattoos, no forgotten ring—"

"Well," said the doctor, "I guess the scoundrels are learning too."

The lieutenant overcame his squeamishness, took the skull carefully into his hands, and examined it. Its teeth were in excellent shape: unspoiled, small, girl's teeth. It even seemed to the detective that they still retained a slight pearly sheen. Three were missing: two canine teeth on the left and one molar on the right.

He examined the jawbone more closely. "Doctor," he said, "look. That molar is only broken off."

Dr. Seifert almost snatched the skull out of Boruvka's hand and looked into the mouth. "Good Lord, Josef!" he said in astonishment. "A good thing you noticed that. Those teeth weren't knocked out, they were *pulled* out. That stump!" And he pointed to the missing molar. "That's exactly how it looks when you try to pull out a tooth and it breaks off in the pliers. Look!"

The lieutenant looked, but the shattered remains of the tooth told him nothing.

"He tried to pry it out. Didn't know what he was doing, and it broke on him. Then he gave up." Dr. Seifert examined the holes where the canine teeth had been. "Just as I thought. These weren't knocked out either," he said. "He pulled them out very neatly. It worked with the canine teeth, but not with the molars."

The lieutenant frowned. "Well, it was a mistake. Those blows to the face and the scalping won't do him a bit of good now. There's only one reason he tried to pull those teeth out."

Dr. Seifert nodded. "Exactly. But Josef, that might have been fifteen years ago. How are you going to track it down now? In fifteen years, they've probably accumulated hundreds of thousands of dental records in the clinics. And back then, they still had private dentists. God only knows where *their* records are."

• • •

It still reminded the detective of something. He sat in his easy chair and tried to read a novel about the founding of a co-operative farm. It was homework in a compulsory course in politics, and besides, the author had taught him German in the Kostelec grammar school. The novel was an exercise in socialist realism and told of how the efforts to build a co-op were sabotaged by a gang of Catholic criminals led by an American agent from Washington who had been sent to the village of Zalesi by the CIA. But the lieutenant's mind wandered back to that unidentified person who, ten or fifteen years ago, had played dentist on a delicate female skull. Once again, it reminded him of something.

He got up, put the novel down, and walked over to the bookshelf. Beneath *The Collected Works of Alois Jirasek* (he had inherited them from his father) was a short row of books belonging to his fifteen-year-old daughter, Zuzana. *Sylva's First Film, Irene Leads the Class, Zdena's Teacher.* Those works had been inherited too, from Zuzana's mother, who was still very energetically alive. The books were dog-eared and well read, whereas the books that the lieutenant had given his daughter on various occasions still looked brand new. *Wuthering Heights, War and Peace, The Gold Bug and Other Stories, Madame Bovary, Gulliver's Travels.* The lieutenant didn't know what had drawn him to the bookshelf. He stood there a while longer, then returned to his chair and the American saboteur in Zalesi. He fell asleep just as the American had managed to destroy the co-op's rabbit hutch, leaving behind him at the scene of the crime a vial of poison bearing the legend "Made in U.S.A."

. . .

The next day at the office, however, he continued to be haunted by the very unprofessional sensation that he had read something relevant somewhere. He was going through a list of people who had gone missing between 1948 and 1953, eliminating the men and putting the young women to one side, when once more he came across the name of Kvetuse Rerichova.

He read through the eleven-year-old report—written by himself—and the more he studied the document, the deeper his frown became. It had been a very, very superficial job. The lieutenant flushed with shame. How could he have been so careless? Of course, he'd been young at the time. But youth is no excuse for negligence. It was true that not much attention was paid to cases like that, except perhaps by the *other* police, to which he did not belong. To make matters worse, he'd been praised for his work. Cold sweat drove away the flush of shame. At the bottom of the report, in red pencil and his own handwriting, were the words: *Case closed; illegal exit to West.*

God! At the time he hadn't even questioned Libuse Rerichova,

Kvetuse's sister. And no one had rapped his knuckles. Nor had he provided a detailed description of the jewelry which the mother said the missing woman had taken with her. All his report said was: "Two rings (gold) and a necklace (silver)." At the bank, he hadn't checked the manager's story. He hadn't bothered to find out if the woman had gone to a dentist, either. How could he have been so sloppy? If his partner, Malek, did slipshod work like that, he'd give him an official reprimand. And he, Boruvka, had been praised for it!

He sighed. That was how it had been in those days. Disappearances were daily occurrences. Most of the missing persons surfaced some time afterwards, in camps in Germany; some didn't, and some showed up ten years later in places like Australia or Argentina. And murders? At the time, murder was treated as a lesser crime; very often they didn't even hang people for it. It was not that he had anything against this reluctance to use "harsh but just" punishments for murderers. But it bothered him that people went to the gallows who weren't even thieves, but just members of a political party. The same party for which the lieutenant had cast his ballot in the remote times when the ballot was still secret.

He realized that his shirt was sticking to his back and his face was burning, as if from a fever. With a sensation of self-reproach, he put the report bearing Kvetuse Rerichova's name back into the file and began to read furiously through the remaining seventy-four entries. So great was his embarrassment that he read the male ones as well.

And still he felt that premonition, or whatever it was.

Suddenly he stuffed everything back into the filing cabinet and quickly left the office.

. . .

Old Mrs. Rerichova was dead by now, and her dark kitchen was occupied by her son Peter and his eighteen-year-old wife. In the narrow room, where the small bookshelf had once stood between two red couches, there was now a crib.

Peter couldn't remember. He had been ten years old at the time.

Kvetuse must have gone to a dentist, but he didn't know which one. Perhaps Liba, the sister, would know. Yes, Liba was married. Her husband was an engineer. They lived in Jamaica Street in Letna.

. . .

There were three nameplates on the door of the flat: Arpad Hruska, L.L.D.; Arnost Hruska, Prof. Eng.; Rudolf Cerveny, Ph.D. A family of intellectuals, thought the lieutenant. But the noises emerging from the other side of the door sounded more like what one might expect to hear in the slums. Two women were shouting at each other: "I've had enough, I tell you, and from now on I forbid you to—" "You can't stop me! It's my own son." "And he's my husband!" A male voice intervened: "Girls, please I beg you—" and a second male voice: "For Christ's sake, I've had it—" Overlapping this cocktail of hysteria, or so the lieutenant guessed, was the screaming of at least two infants, and then the reproachful voice of a third woman: "You've woken up little Jindriska again!"

He rang the doorbell. The voices fell silent. The door was opened by a young woman in a turquoise dressing gown. She had beautiful chestnut-brown hair and a desperate look in her eyes. Several strands of hair had come loose, and she was gathering them away from her face and trying to fix them back in place with a hairpin.

"Yes?"

"Mrs. Hruska?"

"No, I'm Mrs. Cerveny. Do you want to talk to my mother-in-law or my sister-in-law?"

"Your sister-in-law," said the lieutenant. He was embarrassed. "That is, if I'm not interrupting anything."

"Not even the cops could make things worse than they already are," said the pretty but desperate-looking woman, and the lieutenant blushed.

Soon he was sitting alone with another woman in one of the rooms. This woman was older, at least thirty-five. Once, perhaps, she had been pretty too, but now her hair was prematurely gray, and she was overweight and terribly high-strung. They were sitting alone only because the lieutenant had finally resorted to showing his badge to get the red-haired Mrs. Hruska, the engineer, a seven-year-old girl in a dirty dress, and a nine-year-old boy with a bloody nose out of the room.

On the wall were pictures of people in folk costumes, and there was a bookshelf there as well, dominated by a row of Jirasek's *Collected Works* in leather binding. The shelves also contained *Wuthering Heights, War and Peace, Gulliver's Travels,* a row of crime novels, and several other volumes that seemed somehow familiar to the detective. The woman's irritable voice interrupted his reverie on the literary taste of so many multi-generation households.

"So what is it you want to know? What is it I'm supposed to remember? It's been so long."

"Some new evidence has turned up," said the lieutenant, still embarrassed, "indicating that in this case there may not have been an illegal exit from the republic, but—"

"It certainly took you long enough to figure that out, didn't it?" said Mrs. Hruska, with a sarcastic grin. "Eleven years it's been, and we never heard a word from Kvetuse. Do you think she wouldn't even bother telling her own mother where she was? Or that she wouldn't have gone to join her brother? He's got three car-repair shops of his own now, and a house in Florida," she added with undisguised pride. "And poor Mama, when she was still alive, reported it to you several times—"

"I—" The lieutenant tried to interrupt.

"—but you had other problems to worry about, didn't you, and no time to help look for an old woman's poor daughter that some bastard probably did in."

For the second time in this case, the lieutenant had been unjustly identified with a department of the police he did not belong to, and he felt ashamed.

"Just after your sister disappeared I was transferred to another branch. A colleague took over Missing Persons."

"Then he should have realized that something rotten was going on."

"You're quite right. But now some new evidence has come up, and that's why I've come—"

"So get to the point. What do you want to know? The sooner you leave the better. As you may have noticed, things are in a bit of a state around here. Six grown-ups and three children in two rooms—it's enough to drive you crazy."

"Couldn't you join a co-op?" said the lieutenant, and then he bit his lip because he remembered where they had found the skull.

"A co-op? We did—five years ago. They say we're going to get a flat the year after next, but I'll believe it when I see it. That is, if I don't end up in the bughouse before then."

"I only need to know one thing. Do you recall who your sister's dentist was?"

"I do. We've always gone to Dr. Heiser. Now he's working at a clinic in Prague 7. But Kvetuse always had good teeth. Our parents were poor when we were kids. No cakes, no candies. And later we weren't the proper kind of working-class kids either, not like Madam La-di-da, the respectable comrade who looks after these barracks. . . ."

From the next room came the sound of muffled but angry voices. The lieutenant stood up and made an apologetic farewell. He hurried out of the tenement house into the street and look a deep breath of the spring air.

. . .

Dr. Heiser, he discovered, was allowed to have private office hours twice a week. He tended to his patients in a family villa, which was now occupied by the families of two of his sons and a daughter who had remarried. The daughter's first husband slept in the doctor's office. In the attic, under a pile of old rugs, the doctor had a carefully preserved card index of all the patients he had treated since beginning his practice.

The lieutenant found Kvetuse Rerichova's card with its schematic picture of teeth. The dentist had marked three teeth on it: the two canine teeth on the left and a molar on the right. In now-faded ink, he had recorded payment for the filling of three simple cavities.

That evening a very chastened lieutenant took Kvetuse Rerichova's folder out of the Missing Persons file and transferred it to the Unsolved Homicides file. He blacked out his original conclusion with ink and wrote above it in red pencil: *Murdered in May 1952. Murderer as yet unapprehended.*

. . .

Nine months went by. Kvetuse Rerichova's killer remained at large.

At eleven o'clock one morning the telephone rang. The detective lifted the receiver. "Lieutenant Boruvka," he said.

"We've got a murder here, lieutenant. Can you come right away?"

"Give me the address," said the detective automatically. "And don't touch anything."

"It's a Klarov Number One," said the voice. To the detective's ear, it sounded rather jovial. He hoped this wasn't just someone playing a practical joke on him. Such things had happened. But he had a duty to investigate.

"Who's calling?"

"Professor Gebert. There's no particular hurry."

The man hung up. Lieutenant Boruvka had a growing suspicion that this was some kind of silly joke, but even so he woke the drowsing Malek, went into the laboratory and interrupted Dr. Seifert who was eating lunch over the remains of an exhumed leg, picked up the coquettish fingerprint expert Babincakova from the next office, and then with the others got into the Volga squad car and drove off.

Klarov Number One was a gap where the old building had been torn down and foundations were being laid for a new one. A man with a full gray beard stood by the wooden construction fence surrounding the site, along with a girl in jeans wearing her hair in a ponytail, and a young man in blue coveralls and thick glasses. They didn't look like masons.

"I'm Professor Gebert," said the robust, elderly man. "This is Miss Vostra, and this is Jise. They're my colleagues. Miss Vostra discovered the body."

"I hope you left everything just as it was?"

"Yes, of course," said the girl, and opened a door in the wooden fence.

An unexpected sight greeted the lieutenant's eyes. Instead of the usual gang of workers with shovels and bulldozers, there were about ten young men and women working in the excavation. Some of them were digging in the ground with spoons—or at least they looked like spoons to the lieutenant—while others were carefully scraping away at a stone wall that emerged from the clay. At the edge of one pit a young man with a mustache sat dunking a piece of cotton wool in a bowl and delicately wiping off a mud-covered bottle made of green glass and chips of stoneware. Another man was carefully cleaning an object that looked like a court jester's boot. The lieutenant stared at it, amazed.

"Isn't that something?" said Professor Gebert, who was standing behind him. "A perfect Gothic slipper, complete with bells on its toes. There's nothing like it anywhere in the world. Now we're looking for the mate."

The detective came to his senses and asked, "Where's the body?"

"Right this way."

The professor climbed down a ladder into the pit, followed by the lieutenant and the fingerprint expert Babincakova, who immediately began to curse violently. She had come to the police force directly from the army and had just recently finished a course in fingerprinting. Her high-heeled shoes had become stuck in the clay.

The professor led the little group across an exposed section of stone flooring that had obviously been cleared during the excavation to the corner of the stone wall. He stopped and pointed dramatically to a hole broken in the wall, which was made of unfinished stone.

For just an instant, the lieutenant's breath was taken away. A human skull stared at him out of the hole. It wasn't pure white, but brown. On the other hand, it was undamaged.

He looked at the professor, who grinned toothily. "It's murder, lieutenant. It happened some time ago, of course—about six hundred years ago, to be as precise as we can. But it's murder all the same."

"Comrade!" said Malek darkly. "Do you realize that summoning the police on false pretenses is a punishable offense?"

"God—or someone—preserve us!" cried the professor. "I didn't call you here on false pretenses. Our ancestors were not in the habit of burying their dead standing up, nor did they wall them up in their basements. This is a bona fide murder you're looking at. Of course," and he paused, "the murderer really comes under the jurisdiction of the Royal Court of His Majesty Charles the Fourth, Emperor and King by the Grace of God. But since his majesty has been in the bosom of the Lord these six hundred years, the investigation is now a matter for the People's Court of the Capital City of Prague."

"Don't make fun of us, comrade, okay? The statute of limitations on murder is twenty years and that ran out five hundred and eighty years ago, which lays you open to a charge of malicious interference in the work of the Public Security forces."

"Hang on a minute, Pavel," said the lieutenant. The sight had awakened all his investigative instincts, and something else besides.

"There's no need for me here," said Babincakova. "I don't suppose there'll be any fingerprints," and she looked at the archaeology students who were busily scraping away in the dirt with their spoons.

"I don't suppose there will," said the professor.

"Then I'll just take a gander round the site," she said, and in her narrow skirt and high heels she tottered unsteadily towards the young man who was cleaning the bottle.

"Please don't take this amiss," said the professor in a conciliatory tone. "I only thought that, as professionals, you'd be interested. It's not every day you find a five-hundred-year-old corpse."

"Certainly, professor. This is really quite interesting indeed. Pavel," said the lieutenant, turning to Malek, "I believe that in legal terms, this does concern us, even though it's well beyond the statute of limitations." The lieutenant frowned. "Are you absolutely sure this was murder?" he asked, addressing the professor again.

"Look," said the professor, inscribing a wide arc in the air with his finger, "there used to be an ordinary nineteenth-century tenement house here. It was declared unfit for habitation and they tore it down. When they began to dig out the foundations, they found a few medieval coins and other bric-a-brac, so they called us in. We discovered that parts of the foundations go back to the fourteenth century. Beside them we found the pile of glass and stoneware bottles you see over there," and he pointed towards Babincakova, who was already flirting with the mustachioed archaeologist. "It wasn't difficult to deduce how they got there. Before it was regulated, the Vltava River meandered through Prague and also had several 'dead arms' or inlets. The original building here must have stood beside one of those inlets and people walking out of it must have thrown their empty bottles into the water. We found several hundred of them. Why so many bottles? Well, because the building was a tavern. Perhaps one of the ones where King Charles the Fourth, disguised as a commoner, came to get sauced."

The lieutenant looked around. The Vltava was some way off now. He could see the green roof of the Rudolfinum concert hall, and he could hear the screeching of a streetcar braking at the Klarov stop. Dank air was rising off the site, and the skull leered straight at him from the hole broken in the wall. Once again, he felt the tingle of intimation at the back of his neck, a nagging thought, a memory, but he did not know of what.

"And wherever you have taverns, you have brawls. When we uncovered the foundations, I thought it odd that while three of the corners were right angles, that corner over there was rounded. So I authorized my assistants to dismantle it, and Miss Vostra here uncovered this beauty."

The girl with the ponytail smiled happily.

"Can you dig out the whole skeleton?" asked the lieutenant.

"Of course," replied Professor Gebert. "In fact I would say we're obliged to, since you're here. Even though it's beyond the statute of limitations."

. . .

The girl with the ponytail, the young man in the blue coveralls, and the professor very carefully removed the stones from the rounded corner of the wall. The lieutenant's premonition, which seemed to be tugging him in the direction of literature—though he had no idea why—strengthened. Gradually they uncovered the skeleton, and when it was exposed as far as the top of the pelvis, the professor gave a whoop of delight.

"And here we have the *corpus delicti*," he cried, pointing to a rusty object eaten away by the centuries and protruding ragged-edged from the left side of the skeleton's rib cage. "A dagger! He was stabbed in the heart."

Feverishly they kept up their work until they had completely uncovered the skeleton. It was wearing the remains of a belt with a large metal buckle and a leather pouch. Scarcely legible on the buckle was a date, MCCCXLVII, and what was a coat of arms. Breathlessly the professor leaned closer and then turned to the lieutenant. "And we even have a motive. This is the insignia of a royal messenger. Obviously the poor fellow was carrying a lot of money," and he touched the pouch delicately. "He must have stopped by the tavern for a drink and some thieves did him in. They buried the corpse in the cellar, but now, after centuries, as they say—or rather, as they write—the cellar has yielded up its secrets."

. . .

About a week later, the archaeologist invited the lieutenant and his wife for supper. The detective didn't lead much of a social life, and Mrs. Boruvka was worried about what to wear. She was an elegant woman in her thirties, the mother of fifteen-year-old Zuzana and nine-year-old Josef, and she was on the plump side, with a pretty face, gray eyes, black hair, and a beautiful olive complexion inherited from her Italian ancestors. At last she chose a black dress and a large cross of pure gold, although the lieutenant was somewhat reluctant to see his pretty wife decked out in such an ostentatious symbol of Christianity.

He needn't have worried. Professor Gebert's attention was immediately attracted by the cross—and, to tell the truth, by Mrs. Boruvka as well—and he identified it as a work of Italian provenance from the sixteenth century, stylistically related to the famous Cross of Assisi. Mrs. Boruvka was flattered and she reciprocated by admiring the necklace worn by the professor's wife, who was in turn admired—in spirit, not aloud—by the always potentially unfaithful lieutenant. She was a young woman, scarcely twenty-eight, and as it turned out, she had been a student of the professor—far from his best, although almost certainly his favorite. Her necklace had come from the Chod region and was one of those fashioned from Josefine coins by folk artisans, as the professor informed the company, for the wives of well-to-do farmers in the late eighteenth and early nineteenth centuries.

After dinner, as they sat around in armchairs sipping Cointreau and smoking, the professor said, "I wanted to tell you, lieutenant—because I assume it will interest you, despite the statute of limitations—that I've solved the murder of that messenger at the Swan and Star Tavern."

"Seems like you've missed your calling," the lieutenant laughed.

"Wrong," said the professor. "The methods of archaeology and crime detection are remarkably similar. But as it turned out, I needn't have bothered. The murderer was, as they say—or rather, as they write—given a harsh but just punishment. He was drawn and quartered alive, and all four pieces of him were put on display by the Bridge Tower. The only catch is that this harsh but just drawing and quartering was for another murder. But you can only execute someone once, of course, so whatever it was for, he got his just deserts."

The lieutenant looked at his host uncertainly, wondering if perhaps the artful scientist wasn't making the whole thing up as an allegory for a recent report in which a judicial commission had stated that the leader of a particular renegade political faction group was not, in fact, guilty as charged, but that he was otherwise evil and therefore there had been no real miscarriage of justice, even though the formally innocent person in question had already been executed. Mrs. Boruvka, thinking it would be suitable, tried to turn white (it was the lieutenant, rather, who turned pale) and declared, "That's simply awful! Drawn and quartered, you say?"

"Yes. In those days, justice was cruel. But it was just. Times have changed." And the professor winked at the lieutenant.

"How did you come to that conclusion?" said the lieutenant noncommittally, and then realized at once that what he'd said sounded ambiguous.

The professor grimaced—perhaps it was only a habit—and said, "It was easy and logical. The messenger had the year 1347 on his belt. From the old land registries we learned that the name of the tavern was probably the Swan and Star—it's mentioned several times in contemporary sources. Then I looked up the old black books, as they're called—that means the trial records—and I discovered that a certain Matej Ctyrkusy—which, by the way, is a wonderful *nomen omen,* is it not? Makes your blood run cold. Anyway, this Matej Four-piece was the innkeeper of the Swan and Star. He had bought the place in the Year of Our Lord 1335 and was later put to torture and convicted of the murder of his neighbor Cenek Liska, a moneylender from the old town, and sentenced to death. And as I've already said, the chief executioner, called Hynek Urvany—Broke-off Hynek! They all had such wonderful names—and his acolytes cut him in pieces with a saw, first vertically, then horizontally."

"Ludvik, please, couldn't you leave out the details?" said the professor's naturally blonde wife, and then she smiled, but only with her eyes, at Lieutenant Boruvka. Professor Gebert, however, ignored her suggestion.

"I'm a little bothered by this notion of being 'put to torture,'" the professor continued with a grimace, and the lieutenant's suspicion that he was talking in parables increased. Was it possible, the detective wondered—even with the archaeologist's undoubtedly superior education—that so much could be known about the fourteenth century? And did our ancestors really have such names? But the professor continued in an entirely authoritative tone: "First they had to put Matej Ctyrkusy in Spanish boots, then they stretched him on the rack and applied hot coals to his loins, before he would confess. Then he withdrew his confession, so they put him on the rack and applied fire to his loins again, and this time he didn't withdraw his confession. I don't know how it would have turned out if the age of Charles the Fourth had enjoyed our rehabilitational techniques," and he winked at the lieutenant again, so that Boruvka had no choice but to smile back.

"But the circumstantial evidence would suggest," Boruvka replied, "that Matej Ctyrkusy didn't exactly have clean hands. Anyone could have killed that messenger in his tavern. But is it likely that just anyone could have walled him up in the cellar without his knowledge?"

"He was a professional. Anyone can see that," said the professor. "Matej tried to withstand the torture because he knew that something even worse would follow confession. And he wasn't wrong in that. It's true that the head executioner gave him a bottle of spirits before carrying out the punishment—I don't think even the hangman could have enjoyed carrying out an execution like that—and it worked somewhat like an anaesthetic. Even so, before the saw reached his vital organs, Matej Ctyrkusy, according to the black book, lamented in a mighty voice."

"Ludvik," said the professor's wife, "How would you like to change the subject? It's turning my stomach."

The lieutenant had not noticed that part of her body. On the other hand, he had noticed that nestled in the deep décolletage of her dress, and framed by the silver necklace, were beautiful snow-white breasts that went wonderfully well with her naturally blonde hair.

The night was full of specters and foreboding, and Boruvka couldn't help feeling that there was something on the tip of his tongue, something that was stuck just beneath the threshold of full consciousness. He woke up covered in sweat, tossed down his breakfast, and rushed to the office. There, he pulled out the file marked MISSING: KVETUSE RERICHOVA. The word "MISSING" had been crossed out and replaced with the word "MURDERED."

Feverishly, he read through the file. He found what he was looking for. "Two rings (gold) and a necklace (silver)." He jumped up, sat down again, and looked out the window at St. Sidonius. There was not the slightest reason why the two things should have anything to do with one another. The beautiful necklace, made by folk artisans, adorning Mrs. Gebert's lovely breasts. But in a walled-in corner of a medieval cellar, the professor had discovered first a skull and then the whole skeleton of a man murdered six hundred years ago. Perhaps, thought the lieutenant, there did after all exist mystical correspondences between things. Once again, he experienced that unpleasant, involuntary sensation that there was something literary about the case. He too had discovered a skull during another excavation, although it was only twelve years old. And criminology was *not* archaeology. Or was it? The professor's deduction, this necklace, the other necklace—experience had taught him that correspondences between people, murder, and providence never happened according to the rules laid down in detective stories. Sometimes they followed logic, but neither coincidence nor intuition could ever be ruled out. Not even mystical, indefinable things like literary sensations.

Half an hour later he was sitting once more in the flat in Letna, looking at the bookshelves with those familiar volumes, listening to the middle-aged woman who was saying bitterly, "Of course I remember. At the time I was angry with Kvetuse about it, may she rest in peace, because that necklace belonged to me too. And she disappeared with it. Grandmother gave it to both of us. But what of it? I wish it were the only thing in life I'd ever lost," she said wistfully. The lieutenant thought she seemed calmer today.

"Can you describe it to me?"

"It was silver," said Libuse Hruska. "Obviously made by some

village craftsman. It was supposed to be from the eighteenth century. It was made of Theresian coins: there must have been at least
thirty of them, joined with silver wire. A beautiful pattern. Whenever I wore it, people would just stare at it. And at me, too. I
didn't always look the way I do now. But eleven years of marriage
in the same flat with a mother- and father-in-law and a sister-in-
law and three kids doesn't do anything for a person's looks."

"You'd never know it to look at you," said the lieutenant, and
blushed, for there were some lies he could never manage to get
successfully past his lips. "And perhaps the co-op flat will improve
things."

"Maybe. At least they're saying now it'll be ready by the fall."

"Was there something about the necklace by which you could
positively identify it from others like it?"

"Yes, there was," said the gray-haired woman. "All the coins
had Maria Theresa on one side, except for one which had Josef
the Second. Right here in the middle," and she pointed to the
center of her chest, where the professor's wife had those beautiful,
pristine, snowy slopes.

. . .

"Oh, my, lieutenant," said the woman's voice gaily into the telephone when the detective had dialed the professor's number and
asked to be excused for disturbing them. "You're not disturbing
me in the least."

"I'm glad. You know, I was thinking—my wife is having a
birthday soon, and when we were at your place she was very much
taken with your necklace. Do you think I could buy one like it
somewhere?"

For a moment, the woman at the other end was silent.

"Perhaps. I don't know, though. It's a piece of folk art, and
most of the ones like it are probably in the ethnographic museum."

"Where did you get yours?"

"It was—that is, I bought it in an antique shop."

"Which one? I'd like to ask about it."

"Which one? You know, I don't really—I think it may have

been the one on National Street, but I couldn't say for certain any more."

"And when did you buy it? Perhaps they'll still have some like it."

"When . . . ? It must have been about a year ago, or so. They only had the one at the time."

"That doesn't matter," said the lieutenant. "I'll ask anyway. Thank you for your help. And I hope," he added, and he didn't even have to make an effort to have his voice sound sincere, "I hope I'll see you again some day."

"So do I . . . lieutenant."

The detective felt she didn't say this as warmly as she had greeted him.

. . .

The next day, after lunch, he rang the bell at a door with a name-plate on it that read: "Professor Dr. Ludvik Gebert, Member of the Czechoslovak Academy of Sciences." She opened the door, her blonde hair like a halo of sin; she wore a tight-fitting dark blue dress and the necklace was around her neck. The lieutenant noticed that the coin lying right at the foot of those snowy mountains had the image of the Austrian eagle stamped on it.

"Oh, my, lieutenant!" she said again, joyfully. "How did you make out?"

"I didn't," he said mournfully. She invited him to come in.

They sat opposite each other, and the professor's wife poured him a glass of liqueur. Her hair had been given a fresh wave, and a smell of perfume that reminded the lieutenant of something drifted towards him across the coffee table.

The professor's wife looked over at a big grandfather clock. "I still have half an hour's time. Then I have an appointment at the doctor's. Tell me about it."

A smile played around the gray eyes, but they contained a thought, a question.

"They didn't have one," said the lieutenant. "I'm very eager to get one because my wife liked yours so much. They called around to all the other stores, but it's obviously a very rare thing. They told me they hadn't had anything like it for at least five years."

"Is that a fact? I do know it's relatively rare." White fingers with pink nails played with the beautiful necklace, and the coins jingled.

"Perhaps you made a mistake."

"That's possible. I have a very bad memory. And then—my husband is always buying me things. You know—he has a vain wife," and she laughed, but her eyes remained strange.

"Well, I suppose there's nothing to be done," said the lieutenant. "In my profession I don't have much time to comb the stores."

"At least your work isn't boring," said the beautiful young woman, taking the bait which the lieutenant had subtly offered her. "In fact, it must really be very interesting."

"Not as interesting as your husband's work, I'm afraid. Even though—believe it or not—I'm working on a case now that is very much like the one your husband solved. I mean the murder that took place in Charles the Fourth's time."

"You don't say!"

"A skull was unearthed at a construction site on the outskirts of the city. It wasn't as old, of course, only about twelve years. It was a female skull, not a male. And I've managed to identify it. Her name was Kvetuse Rerichova. She disappeared twelve years ago. Someone murdered her."

"That's astounding!"

"Not really. My main concern now is to find her killer, because this crime is well within the statute of limitations and the murderer may well be alive and at large. And if he's murdered somebody once. . . . But I only have a single clue, and that's led me nowhere."

"Oh, but you'll solve it, I'm sure. Would you like another drink?"

The professor's wife leaned over to reach the bottle, and her necklace swung like a pendulum.

"That's interesting," said the lieutenant.

"What's interesting?"

The young woman followed the direction of the detective's glance and interpreted it inaccurately. She laughed.

"Have you noticed," said the lieutenant, "that all the coins on your necklace have portraits of Maria Theresa, except for one which has Josef the Second?"

"D'you mean this one?" said the young woman, and with her white fingers she picked up the coin that was resting on the spot where the white hills vanished beneath the dark blue neckline.

"Yes," sighed the lieutenant.

"Look on the other side."

She leaned forward towards the lieutenant so that he could see properly. The scent of sandalwood wafted around him but, even so, he resisted the temptation to look at her breasts. He examined the coin closely.

Suddenly he straighted up. The young woman stared at him in surprise. "Where did you get it?" he asked unhappily.

"But I've already told you."

"I *know* what you told me. What I want to know now is *who* gave it to you."

She was silent.

"Your husband? I certainly hope it wasn't!" cried the lieutenant almost desperately.

The blonde woman took a drink, then looked searchingly into the lieutenant's eyes. The lieutenant, who was usually shy, returned her stare.

"You're investigating a murder, aren't you?" she said quietly. The lieutenant had meanwhile managed to relax. No, the necklace had not been a gift from the sympathetic professor. He had, of course, showered his young wife with jewelry—but young wives with older husbands remember the origin of their jewelry better than anything else.

"Yes," he said, "I'm investigating a murder. But don't worry. I won't tell your husband."

Once again there was a long pause while her eyes made searching enquiries. This time she glanced away. She might not have been the professor's best student, but she was clearly the prettiest and she was certainly very intelligent as well. Or perhaps she was merely clever. When she spoke, her voice trembled slightly. "Why are you interested in where I got my necklace? I mean, if it's a murder you're investigating."

"I don't think I need to go into detail. I think you can work that out for yourself."

The young woman shuddered. Once again, she took the beautiful silver object in her white fingers. "This clue of yours . . ." The lieutenant nodded.

The professor's wife let go of the necklace as though it had suddenly become red-hot. She turned pale.

"I feel ill," she said, and took a sip of her drink. Then, more hopefully, she went on, "But perhaps it's a mistake. The murderer could have sold it—after all, it was twelve years ago and—he—" she hesitated, and the whiteness that reminded the lieutenant, in his dreams, of the beautiful skull gave way to a blush—"he could have bought it in an antique shop."

She shook her head. The hope was extinguished; the flush died.

"I feel as though I've just reached out and touched something horrible in the dark," she said and tears began streaming down her face. But they were tears of horror more than anguish. "And he looks—and behaves completely—and I—"

"It happens all the time," said the lieutenant. "Particularly with murderers who kill for money, like him. Of course," and he thought for a moment as he remembered something the blonde woman's husband had said, "in his case there was a clear pathological aspect to it. I mean more obviously than usual, because every murderer is sick."

"But he really does behave—just the way you'd expect—expect a bank manager to behave."

The lieutenant, however, was not listening. He was absorbed in his own thoughts.

"The fact that he cut her up into pieces and even boiled the head and scraped away all the fleshy parts . . . What did you say your—friend—did for a living?"

He looked at the blonde woman.

Her complexion was green and she was just rising from the couch. Then she rushed out somewhere into the hall and for a long time the lieutenant sat in the room alone, his shame and sadness mitigated only by a very tiny sense of satisfaction. That the girl who twelve years ago had been fed up with everything would now finally be—what, really?

. . .

It was a case full of strange correspondences. When the lieutenant went to see Libuse, to tell her that her sister's murderer had been arrested, she was no longer living in the flat on Jamaica Street. She had moved, the concierge told him, to a new co-operative flat.

"Where?" asked the lieutenant, a sense of foreboding tingling at the back of his neck.

"Krc," said the concierge.

So the detective told Libuse nothing about where they had found the beautiful skull and said only that he had based all his deductions on the coin bearing the likeness of Josef the Second. But Libuse was not really interested in his deductions.

"A nice flat? You call this a new flat?" she said bitterly when the lieutenant praised their new one-bedroom suite. "Just take a look!" And she led the lieutenant into the bathroom, where she demonstrated some of the features of the apartment. The bathroom was too small for both a bathtub and a sink, so the inventive architect had designed a washbasin that could be attached to the edge of the tub when no one was having a bath. When the washbasin was in place, it was impossible to get into the bathtub, which otherwise was long enough to lie down in, as long as you could put your knees up around your ears.

"At least you have the whole flat to yourselves."

"Look, lieutenant or whatever you are," said Libuse, "when I got married, I was twenty-five. Now, when I'm thirty-seven, I finally have an apartment on my own and an eleven-year-old daughter. She's *already* mad about boys, and by the time she's seventeen at the lastest she'll be in trouble and then we'll have three generations crowded around the detachable washbasin all over again."

The detective said nothing. He thought about the manager of the savings bank who, because of numerous extenuating circumstances (the time elapsed since the crime, no other criminal offenses, a wonderful political record, a long history of dedicated Party activity, and an immediate and full confession) would get, he guessed (accurately, as it turned out), no more than fifteen years, so that in relative security (he would certainly continue to cooperate with the prison authorities) he would await his forty-eighth year, or more likely the nearest amnesty. Whereas the driver's mate who had committed an act invented by a perverse Mother Nature upon his dead wife's body had, lacking Party connections, swung at the end of a rope.

"So I'll have this flat to myself for six, seven years at the most. And then I'll be forty-four," Libuse said bitterly.

The lieutenant could think of nothing to say. He looked around and on the walls saw the same figures in their folk costumes, and Jirasek in his leather bindings was on the bookshelf, a gift edition of Nemcova, detective novels, *Wuthering Heights, The Gold Bug and Other Tales, Jane Eyre, War and Peace.*

"And then my boy will get married, naturally to some stupid girl who has nowhere to live. . . ."

The lieutenant rose to his feet guiltily.

"Why am I telling you all this?" said the gray-haired, thirty-seven-year-old woman, rising as well. "It's not your fault. And it was nice of you to take the trouble to avenge our Kvetuse's death. I hope they hang the creep. He deserves to be drawn and quartered, the bastard."

But the lieutenant knew that punishment in the people's democratic states was no longer cruel, only harsh and just. And if a person cooperates with the Party and doesn't commit anything worse than murder. . . .

He shuddered. At what Libuse had wanted to happen to the murderer. At all those correspondences.

That night he couldn't sleep.

. . .

Next day, towards evening, he sat in his room and, through the open door, watched while his teenage daughter, Zuzana, struggled over her Russian homework. He marveled at how they had come by this little love nest, through circumstances that were almost mystical: the landlady, although she was only forty-seven, had suddenly died, so that when Zuzana was little they had not just a back room, but a whole flat to live in. What luck that had been! How lucky he had been all his life, in fact. Perhaps the world wasn't such an evil place after all, even though many evil things took place in it. On the other hand, there were so many wonderful things to compensate. He looked at the teenager over her homework, at the bookshelf behind her and the rows of volumes. There it was again, that strange sensation at the back of his neck. He stood up, walked into the next room, and pulled a book off the shelf. Yes. He had seen it in the new flat in Krc. *The Gold Bug and Other Tales*. He opened it up and read:

I asked myself—"Of all melancholy topics, what, according to the *universal* understanding of mankind, is the *most* melancholy?" Death—was the obvious reply. "And when," I said, "is this most melancholy of topics most poetical?" . . . "When it most closely allies itself to *Beauty*: the death, then, of a beautiful woman is, unquestionably, the most poetical topic in the world . . ."

The lieutenant didn't understand that. He remembered a photograph of Kvetuse, a pretty blonde girl with a beautiful, long face that had been transformed into a beautiful, long cranium. He leafed through a few pages and read again, shuddering:

With a shriek I bounded to the table, and grasped the box that lay upon it. But I could not force it open; and, in my tremor, it slipped from my hands, and fell heavily, and burst into pieces; and from it, with a rattling sound, there rolled out some instruments of dental surgery, intermingled with thirty-two small, white, and ivory-looking substances that were scattered to and fro about the floor.

His whole body trembled. The beautiful white skull stared at him through the open window. I'll not encounter anything more terrifying than that, he thought, not after this. He turned a few more pages and read again: ". . . the strange anomaly of life . . . feelings, with me, *had never been* of the heart, and my passions *always were* of the mind"—but he didn't understand that either. Still, it horrified him. How could passion—and emotion—from reason. . . .

He didn't understand it for a long time. Not, in fact, until he saw those two dead girls in the long, green grass.

Ornament in the Grass

They were lying side by side in the tall, succulent grass, wearing light summer blouses and short skirts; they couldn't have been more than sixteen years old. Their breasts had been riddled by gunfire. Their eyes had probably seen the murderer but now saw nothing at all, though the two girls seemed to be staring glassily at each other. Their slender legs and arms, lying askew, created an almost aesthetic image in the grass. They were in a meadow near an evergreen woods that smelled of pine cones. On one side the meadow sloped down towards a river, from which a crowd of people in bathing suits and several soldiers in summer uniforms had come running. Uniformed police officers were holding the crowd back at some distance. It was June—1968—and the entire scene was lit by a glaring noonday sun.

"What made you come this way if you were looking for blueberries?" asked the lieutenant, turning back to a terrified old woman who was sitting in the grass, threading a rosary bead by bead through her fingers. "Couldn't you have gone straight from Oresi into the woods along the road?"

"It was the soldiers turned me back," said the old woman in a high, shrill voice. "So I cuts across the meadow from the river— and just about trips over—over these poor wee girls."

"Do you know who they are?"

"I can't say. I can't bear looking at them."

"Go ahead and look," said Sergeant Malek. "You'll have to sooner or later, anyway."

"Just a moment, Pavel," the lieutenant interrupted him. "Come over here."

He showed the sergeant two bullets the ballistics expert, Jandacek, had found in the grass.

"Nine-millimeter," said Malek, glancing at the soldiers in the crowd of onlookers. The uniformed policemen were still holding them all back at a respectable distance. "From an army pistol?"

"I doubt it," said Jandacek. "One of them caught four, the other one three, and they were both shot in the chest. Which means they were both facing where the shots came from. Try firing a pistol four times in a row fast enough to make a line of bullet holes that's practically horizontal. And why didn't the other one try to run away? If she had, she would have been hit in the back."

"So it was a submachine gun," growled Malek. He glared at the soldiers again, and the lieutenant saw that, as usual, a premature conclusion was forming in the sergeant's head.

Lieutenant Boruvka turned back to the old woman. "Are you sure you couldn't stand to look at them, mother?"

"Jesus, Mary, and Josef, no!" wailed the woman, and she covered her eyes with the hand that was holding her rosary.

The lieutenant looked around. Not far away, the crowd of half-dressed onlookers was listening intently. Then a hand went up. It belonged to a soldier in a wrinkled uniform.

"Something you want?" the lieutenant called out.

"Corporal Hemele, sir," the soldier bawled in brisk, military fashion.

"Come over here, corporal."

"Yes sir, comrade lieutenant, sir!" the soldier bawled again. The lieutenant felt a little conspicuous. The soldier halted the regulation three steps in front of him, stood stiffly at attention, and shouted, though somewhat less loudly, "Permission to speak, sir. I can identify these girls. Their names are Jarmila Machova and Jaroslava Novak."

The young man was about nineteen, roughly shaved, with a low forehead and sincere eyes.

"You may—ah—stand at ease," said the detective awkwardly. When the corporal had responded, the lieutenant, to bolster his dignity, barked at the crowd the way the soldier had: "I want you all to move away from the scene of the crime, is that clear? The evidence is getting trampled. All of you, back to the river. But no one leave!"

Boruvka led the young man over to the edge of the field, and they both sat on the grass. "I went on a date with Jarmila," Corporal Hemele explained. "About a week ago."

"And did you ever go on a date with the other one—Jaroslava?"

"Well, it's kind of embarrassing."

"What do you mean?"

"These girls were just fooling around."

"Fooling around?"

"I was right over there in the woods with Jarmila," and the corporal nodded towards the dark shadow of fir trees just beyond the green meadow, "and just when we were about to, you know, get down to it, suddenly this other one, Jaroslava, crawls out of the bushes and she—they—"

"They what?"

"They started saying these stupid things, that's all."

"What kind of things?"

"Stupid things, I don't know how to describe it."

"Well," said the lieutenant, "you can hardly expect girls that young to say anything wise. Can you—reproduce what they were saying?"

"Well—Jarka said their parents never gave them any money so both of them had started, you know, doing it. Hooking. They said they charged fifteen crowns a throw, but if I'd take on both of them at once they'd only charge me twenty crowns altogether."

The lieutenant felt the blood rise to his head. He looked around at the girls' bodies lying as if deliberately arranged, and he remembered the pure faces frozen in expressions of terror. "And—and what about you?" he asked. "Did you give them the—twenty crowns?"

"That's what I'm trying to tell you. It was all just stupid talk."

"So you don't think they meant it?"

"No, not really." The corporal's answer sounded evasive. The lieutenant, somewhat recovered from his shock, was about to say that he didn't understand, but fortunately, he remembered an expression that seemed more appropriate.

"Could you be more precise?"

"Okay, it was like this. I gave them the twenty crowns, right? I mean, they were both pretty girls and they looked like they needed the money. But instead of, well—" The corporal swallowed. "I mean, they just took the twenty and they—" He swallowed again. "I don't know how to describe it—"

The lieutenant felt hot behind the ears. He was sure the corporal was about to describe an act he had heard about but never engaged in himself.

"Try to be more precise," he said again.

"They gave me a kind of lecture."

"A lecture?"

"Like a sermon. They said it was a sin. They said if young people have sex too early it makes them irresponsible, or some dumb thing like that—I don't mean the irresponsibility, I mean they were just making fun of me. And when I asked for my twenty crowns back they said it was like a fine for bad behavior, and they said they were going to put it in the poorbox in church or give it to the Fund of the Republic, they hadn't decided which. And then they ran away."

"That was silly," said Lieutenant Boruvka. "And also unbecoming."

"It was a stupid joke," said Corporal Hemele. "But, like I say, they were okay girls," he added, obviously remembering the popular dictum about speaking no ill of the dead. "They were just a bit too smart for their own good."

The lieutenant was silent. He watched gloomily as the uniformed policemen loaded the dead girls into an ambulance, under Dr. Seifert's direction. He turned to the corporal again and noticed that he was in combat uniform. "Are you out on a pass today?"

"No, we're here on maneuvers."

"Why aren't you with your unit?"

"They gave us time off for a break."

"When was that?"

"About—0900 hours."

The lieutenant looked at his watch. "It's one p.m. now."

"I know."

"Do your breaks usually go that long?"

The corporal hesitated, then said, "Comrade lieutenant, I don't know if I'm allowed to tell you or not. We were given an order, sort of."

"I understand. Where's your commander?"

• • •

Lieutenant Silny, commander of the armored personnel carrier, was sitting on the grass at the far side of the meadow.

"Our orders were to move the platoon from the barracks in Ouhlice over the bridge on the Uplava, through the Ul woods and the village of Oresi, and up to Hratvi Hill, where we were supposed to camouflage the transport and await further orders."

"What time did you leave Ouhlice?"

"At 0812."

"I see," said the lieutenant. "I don't know anything about armored personnel carriers. I was with the tank corps. But I assume these carriers can travel faster than that."

"Their average speed is forty-five kilometers an hour," said the officer, who obviously liked exactness and precision.

"Then it seems you didn't cover the whole route at that speed.

From Ouhlice here to the bridge over the Uplava is about four kilometers and it's now one in the afternooon, so—"

"There was—" The officer hesitated. "We had a breakdown."

"Is that why you gave the crew some time off?"

"Affirmative."

"And the problem's repaired now?"

"Affirmative. It wasn't anything serious."

"But the repairs took you more than four hours?"

The lieutenant looked sharply at the officer, and the transport commander suddenly seemed less sure of himself and his facts.

"Well—then there was a contravention of my orders," he said uncertainly. "I had to investigate."

"What happened?"

"Three soldiers—against my orders—left the vehicle and went into the woods."

"Why?"

"To pick blueberries," said the officer.

The lieutenant said nothing. He could hear the river murmuring quietly in the distance. Memories of his own military service flashed through his mind. He seemed to feel again the deadly boredom of waiting around on the tank exercise grounds, and how they had found relief in gluttony. They had picked wild strawberries, blueberries, raspberries, anything they could find, not because they were hungry but because there was nothing else to do. He remembered how once—on the summit of Okrouhlice, out of sheer boredom—he had eaten raw mushrooms that Sergeant Krajta had sworn were edible no matter how you prepared them. Sergeant Krajta had been wrong and the lieutenant had spent a pleasant week in the garrison infirmary, where each evening the joyfully indisposed soldiers had talked until long after darkness had descended. Sergeant Krajta had been in the infirmary too, for the clap. Some years later, during a reserve army training session, Krajta had been arrested by the Military Secret Police and sentenced to four years for incitement to rebellion, which he was alleged to have committed by reading the reservists an irreverent story about army life written in his own hand. As for the lieutenant, the mushroom poisoning had left no permanent damage, and after his refreshing week in the infirmary he had returned to his boring vigil on the tank exercise grounds, and to eating blueberries.

He snapped out of his reverie. "Which soldiers were they, comrade lieutenant?" he asked.

Once again Lieutenant Silny found himself on firm, factual ground. "Corporal Hemele, Lance-Corporal Ruzicka, and Private Koubek."

. . .

Now Lance-Corporal Ruzicka was sitting on the grass with the lieutenant.

"Like, we just wanted to go to the woods to get some sleep," he said. "The sun was too hot down by the river and anyways they could see us. So we said to hell with orders—" He paused, then continued gloomily, "Comrade Lieutenant Silny says we're going to get at least twelve nights with a blanket because it was a combat situation."

"The comrade lieutenant is right," said the detective. "An order is an order."

"Yeah, but when—"

The lance-corporal didn't finish saying what he had on the tip of his tongue.

"But when what?"

"I mean, we were desperate to get some sleep."

The detective knew this was not what the soldier had been about to say. He had also noticed that Lance-Corporal Ruzicka hadn't mentioned anything about blueberries. He changed the subject.

"Did you know either of the two dead girls?"

Reluctantly the lance-corporal said, "Yeah, I knew them both." "How well?"

"Not all that well—but well enough. I had a date once with Jaroslava."

The lieutenant felt an uneasy sense of *déjà vu*. "What about the other one, Jarmila, did you even have a—a meeting with her?"

"No. Well, actually, they both came."

"On the date?"

"It was pretty embarrassing, if you want to know the truth."

"Could you be more precise?" asked the lieutenant.

"I was with Jarka over there in the woods." Ruzicka nodded towards the dark patch of fir trees beyond the green meadow. "And when we were just about ready to get down to it—like, I mean nothing had happened yet but it looked pretty promising— all of a sudden Jarmila steps out of the bushes and—"

The lieutenant listened to the story he had already heard once. When Lance-Corporal Ruzicka concluded his tale with, "They took their twenty and beat it," the lieutenant asked:

"Where did you first meet these girls?"

"Me?" The lance-corporal thought a moment, and the process that began to take place behind his wide face was almost visible to the lieutenant's X-ray vision.

"Don't keep anything back," said the detective. "Remember you're speaking to a member of the security forces; if you lie to me it could be treated as perjury."

"I met one of them on guard duty," said the lance-corporal.

The lieutenant was astonished. "On guard duty?"

"I guess I'm in deep shit."

"Anything you say here will remain strictly between you and me," said the lieutenant. "Matters of internal army discipline are none of my business."

"Really?" The face of the lance-corporal brightened somewhat. "Well, it was by the ammunition dump, you know? It's a shitty duty to draw. One circuit takes almost fifteen minutes. Anyway, that's where I met Jarka."

"Tell me how it happened."

"I'm walking back and forth like a jerk—I mean, according to regulations. There's a full moon so I can see pretty good, and suddenly this girl in a white blouse comes out of the bushes and starts walking towards me. Now, according to regulations I've got to shout 'Halt!' or 'Stop or I'll shoot!' but it seems like a dopey thing to say with the moon shining down to beat the band

and this girl walking straight for me. So I just point my gun at her—more like a joke, really—and I say, 'Hey, hold on there, what's your name?' and she says 'Jarmila,' and I say, 'Don't be crazy, I'm here on guard duty and that's an ammunition dump over there and if they catch you here you're in real trouble,' and all she says is, 'Hey, what's your name?' So I say, 'Franta,' and she says, 'Hey, Franta, why don't you put down that tommy-gun? I've been watching you for half an hour and you're a good-looking fellow. Come on over here and make love to me in the bushes.' And I say, 'You're out of your mind. I'm on guard duty.' And she says, 'Come on, it'll be fantastic!' and I say, 'No way, not when I'm on guard duty.' 'So meet me in the U1 woods tomorrow,' she says, and then she was gone. So the next day, just in case she really meant it, I went over to the U1 woods, and Jarmila was waiting in the bushes. And that's where she played that dumb joke that cost me a twenty."

· · ·

Private Koubek told the same story about being on guard duty by the munitions dump, except that it had been Jaroslava who came to him. By this time the lieutenant's thigh was black and blue where he'd been pinching himself in disbelief. "And what happened when you went to meet her in the woods?" he asked.

"It was embarrassing," said the private, and the detective heard yet a third description of the girls' behavior. This incident too ended with the misspent twenty crowns.

"Give me a break, Josef!" Sergeant Malek said later. "All three of them? Burned by the same trick? And did each of them know it happened to the others?"

"They claim they didn't. And I tend to believe them. Would you advertise a thing like that if it happened to you?"

"No, but I bet it leaked out somehow," Malek retorted and then he said with absolute certainty, "They're lying! They're lying because they found out they'd all been had, and they're in collusion. Don't you see?"

"See what?"

"Remember what Janacek said? That those girls were done in by a submachine gun? These three galoots saw the girls somewhere, crawled into the woods after them, and shot them to get even. They were raving mad at them. And they bamboozled the commander into thinking they'd gone there to have a sleep."

"You mean to pick blueberries."

"See what I mean? There's even a contradiction in their testimony!" The lieutenant was well aware of that, but he pointed out, "Pavel—the first one, Corporal Hemele, *volunteered* to identify the girls. . . ."

Malek's complexion darkened, and he slapped his forehead violently.

"Sorry, Josef!"

Still, experience had taught the lieutenant that in his line of work anything was possible. Just to be on the safe side, he decided to have the trio's guns sent for analysis.

. . .

As Boruvka drove to Oresi—the home of the slain girls—his mind wandered back to other memories of his military service, now so pleasantly post factum. Once upon a time he too had been assigned sentry duty at a munitions dump, and on his rounds he had unexpectedly been taken by a powerful fit of sneezing. When he had walked around the building and come back to the same place, he heard a weak cry. He released the safety catch on his weapon and, unlike the too-civil lance-corporal, shouted the mandatory formula into the starry darkness: "Step out here or I'll shoot!" Whereupon a reply came back from the starry darkness: "I can't step out, you fool! You come over here!" It was a woman's voice. With the safety catch still off, and confused because he couldn't recall what the regulations said about a situation like this, he cautiously approached the bushes the voice was coming from. Then he saw them: Comrade Captain Kohn and the wife of First Lieutenant Pinkas, both of them lacking certain items of clothing and obviously engaged in something they had no right to engage in, at least not with each other. As he wondered what to do, he remembered the standing orders: *The sentry shall summon the commander of the guard.* "I'll summon the commander of the guard," he said. "Oh, for God's sake!" said the woman, who was lying underneath the apparently helpless captain. "Don't be insane, man. Don't do anything crazy. Look, what's your name?" And the lieutenant—then a sergeant—forgot about standing orders for a moment and, remembering a folksy legend about the composer Leos Janacek, wondered if the captain too had suffered a stroke while making love.

"Sergeant Boruvka!" he announced crisply, and then, "Are you all right, comrade captain?" The captain was still alive, because he groaned, and Mrs. Pinkas said, "You just scared the hell out of us when you sneezed. My God, it was like the dump exploded! Look, Boruvka, can you get a message to Lieutenant Sadar? Tell him to get here on the double and bring an injection, you know what I mean?" Boruvka had no idea what she meant, but he suddenly realized the stupidity of his first remark: that night the commander of the guard was not First Lieutenant Kamen, who had suddenly been taken ill, but First Lieutenant Pinkas. "Leave it to me, Comrade Mrs. Pinkas!" He reengaged the safety catch on his weapon and marched briskly off into the blackness surrounding the munitions dump; his shift was over in five minutes anyway.

Back in the guardhouse he waited until the commander of the guard had gone to the bathroom, and then—his heart pounding—dialed the number of the infirmary, where, fortunately, Lieutenant Sadar, M.D., was on duty. "I don't know. I guess there's something wrong with them," he faltered, with a backward glance at the door in case the commander was coming. "They're lying on top of each other, like they were stuck together—" "Oh, shit!" Dr. Sadar interrupted. "You say it's by the munitions dump?" "Yeah." "When's your next shift?" "In two hours, but I can trade off with someone else, or—don't worry, I'll arrange it somehow." So Sergeant Krajta, who was game for any mischief, simulated a gall-bladder attack, Boruvka volunteered as a replacement, and half an hour later he saw Dr. Sadar emerge from a starry shadow behind the munitions dump, his little black bag in hand. Boruvka led the doctor to the bushes, then posted himself as lookout. Five minutes later the doctor emerged from the bushes and said, "Back to your figure skating!" And as the lieutenant was setting out at a brisk walk on his circuit around the dump, he saw two figures in the dim glow of starlight, a man and a woman, flitting out of sight.

. . .

Half an hour later he was at the collective farm in Oresi, sitting in the office of the chairman, Josef Novak. The chairman's eyes were red from crying, but he had regained his self-control. "I often thought," he said, "that Slavka—that's what we called her—would end up badly one day. But I never expected this."

"What made you think that?"

"Frankly, she wasn't much good for anything. She was lazy; all she ever did was listen to pop records and roam about by herself at night. A couple of times I gave her a good thrashing. But you know how it is—her mother was taken away when she was three and I'm always too busy to spend any time with her." And the chairman went on to describe for the lieutenant's benefit a life story that might have been lifted straight from the socialist realist novels he had once read to help him get to sleep: a Party functionary who devoted so much of his time to the Party and the collective farm that he had none left for his children. "And Franta, my boy, is just the same. Bums around the country, work-shy. No, comrade, my children didn't turn out very well. But this—"

The chairman looked out the window at a building across the courtyard. A brand-new imported car was parted in front of it. Tears were streaming down his cheeks.

"We'll do what we can," said the lieutenant.

"I know you will, comrade. But it's too late. I should have taken my belt to her a little oftener. But I will with my boy, believe me. As soon as Franta comes back—I know it may not be the proper progressive approach, but I remember how my father—"

. . .

Jarmila Machova's parents had a distinctly different view of their daughter, one that did not coincide in the least with what the soldiers had told the lieutenant about the girl's behavior. An exemplary daughter, worked hard at school, wanted to be a doctor and all her teachers backed her up in that. Yes, perhaps she'd been a bit frivolous, but when you looked at other girls her age—and she was even a—The weeping Mrs. Machova lowered her voice to confide this to the embarrassed lietuenant: Jarmilka had had some sort of problem, she said, so they'd taken her to the doctor and the doctor had said, "I'm sorry, but I can't give her a proper examination." "And stupid me," Mrs. Machova sobbed, "I said, 'For the love of Jesus, doctor, is it something serious?' and the doctor said, 'It's unusual in this day and age, but it's hardly serious. Your daughter's still a virgin. As for her problem—we'll give her some pills and she'll be right as rain in no time.' So he did, and Jarmila was as healthy as a horse again. Oh, lieutenant! If I knew the monster who did this, I'd take these hands and I'd—"

.   .   .

It wrung the lieutenant's heart to think of that beautiful suntanned girl—a girl who might have been a doctor—lying in the grass like a picture. He could hear a radio somewhere outside, and Jarmila's younger sister, now sitting in front of him, was also suntanned and might have been pretty. At that moment they all seemed beautiful to him, just because they were all so young.

The girl was crying her heart out.

"And this Frantisek Novak," the old detective was saying quietly, "was she in love with him?"

The girl shook her head, but she could hardly bring herself to speak. "Jarka—" she sobbed, "Jarka didn't find him too interesting. She was kind of stringing him along. Once he got drunk and climbed through a window into our house. Fortunately the parents weren't home, so we poured a bucket of water on him and he sobered up. Once he even threatened to kill her. He was drunk then too. He drinks quite a bit. But I don't think he really meant it. Franta talks a lot. That's another reason Jarka didn't like him."

She began to sob uncontrollably again. Despite his long years of service the lieutenant was not a callous man. Suddenly he had a—a premonition—God knows what—that this murder, this kind of murder, had implications wider than a teenager's jealous revenge. He had no idea what the implications were. Not then, with the weeping fifteen-year-old desperately listening to the hit song drifting into the room through the begonias outside the window.

.   .   .

So he had all but excluded Franta Novak from the list of suspects when an anonymous phone call reminded him of that delinquent son of the collective-farm chairman. But the call didn't come until Monday morning. On the Sunday evening, before going back to Prague, he paid a visit to the army barracks in Ouhlice, where at his request the commanding officer, Major Kadavy, had the whole garrison fall in on the parade ground. In the honey-colored light of the June evening, a formation of some two hundred men (or so they were called in military parlance) stood at attention before the lieutenant. He addressed them briefly:

"Comrades! An inhuman act has taken place near your garrison. Two young girls have been murdered by an unknown assailant and it is now our responsibility to help ensure that the perpetrator is tracked down and given the punishment he merits." Whenever the lieutenant spoke in any official capacity he resorted, against his will, to the appropriate vocabulary. That evening, however, he suddenly found himself abandoning his habitual style. "What is there in this world that can be sadder than life?" he asked. At this Major Kadavy, who was standing slightly behind him, raised his eyebrows. "Death, comrades," the lieutenant went on, with a feeling that he had read this somewhere before. "And when is death saddest of all? When it touches beauty and innocence. So the death of an innocent young girl, a girl who might have become a doctor—or the wife of any one of you, for that matter, the mother of your children and therefore the giver of new life—such a death, comrades, is the saddest of all. I appeal to you: would all of you who knew the girls personally, and who want to see the murderer caught, please step forward!"

The honey-colored sun lit the nominally shaved faces of these nominal men, and the lieutenant knew that his words, at least partially liberated from official diction, and coming, it almost seemed, from somewhere outside him, had had an impact. Heels clicked together and two men stepped forward from the ranks.

· · ·

In the next thirty minutes, the lieutenant listened to another couple of stories that, aside from a few minor variations, were indistinguishable from the three tales he had heard on the grass that day. Stories of the strange summer games of the two girls who had pretended to be prostitutes and had turned out to be preachers; of a girl who had wanted to become a doctor and who had been a creature called—in a beautiful dead language—a *virgo intacta*.

As he listened to the stories he thought about the follies of youth. Once, a terribly long time ago, he and Smiricky, who played tenor sax in the Kostelec students' orchestra, had gone to a village called Destna in the Eagle Mountains and posed as members of the famous Karel Vlach Jazz Band. The idea had been to show off in front of a similar pair of girls, Bozena and Jitka. At the dance afterwards they had played a rather miserable imitation of Goodman's solo from "Sing, Sing, Sing!" on out-of-tune clarinets. A tipsy villager called Klepetar, a fanatical partisan of Czech folk music, had thrown a beer glass at them, triggering such an explosion of passionate hatred that they had barely managed to escape by running down a steep hill, scraping their knees on the way and breaking one of the two clarinets. If that had happened in America, Boruvka reflected, they would probably have been tarred and feathered. A silly, pointless memory, but it stayed with the lieutenant all the same. And he thought about that mysterious, uniquely human combination: the remarkable intelligence of the brain, mingled with the folly that so often overpowers it in someone who is very young.

And that premonition—try as he might to chase it away, for such phenomena were out of place in his work—burdened his soul again. He shook his head in another effort to rid himself of this irrational psychological interference.

. . .

"Take a look at them!" said Sergeant Malek, who was standing by his side. "They're buggering off back to where they came from!"

The hideous, flat gray machines were rattling slowly along the road towards them in the moonlight. White Soviet stars shone bleakly on their armor plating.

"Maneuvers, my foot!" said Malek. "It sure took them long enough to see they're not needed here. Good riddance!"

The lieutenant felt as if a stone were being lifted off his heart. So it was true: the Soviet army had at long last concluded its seemingly endless military exercises, and was leaving. The country and all the new, promising changes were safe now. The newspapers were no longer what they had been less than a year ago, and a case like that of Miss Peskova . . . who could say? Perhaps it would be reported in the papers these days. A great hope swelled in the lieutenant's heart. The new, long-nosed first secretary, Alexander Dubcek, appeared to his inner eye. He was making a speech in the Old Town Square and the lieutenant, standing at his open window on a summer evening, could hear the sound of a large crowd cheering. He felt an affection for the long-nosed man that he'd never harbored for any previous first secretary.

. . .

The telephone call came first thing the next morning, almost before the lieutenant had a chance to settle into his swivel chair.

"Mr. Boruvka?" said a voice. "I got something important to tell you about that double murder in Oresi. Chairman Novak owns a pistol. They gave him a license back in the fifties when the son-of-a-bitch helped drive out the so-called kulaks. And his precious son Franta sometimes borrows the pistol. The old man doesn't know about it because his head's too full of meetings and five-year plans. And Franta was nuts over one of those girls, Jarmila Machova. So maybe you should take a look at that pistol, lieutenant."

There was a click and the telephone went dead. It wasn't hard to guess why the anonymous caller was so eager to supply information. The accusation was certainly not relevant: the deed had been done with a submachine gun, according to the experts. But the old detective knew that in a murder case no lead, however improbable, must be neglected. After all, even experts sometimes turned out to be unaccountably wrong. And sometimes—he knew this, too, from bitter experience—the experts changed their minds when circumstances turned up that were thought to be more important than evidence. At least, until recently they had. He went to see the chairman again.

. . .

"I do have a pistol, comrade," said the chairman, "and the ammunition for it. But I've never used it."

"Show it to me."

The chairman reached into the bottom drawer of his desk and turned pale.

"It's not here!"

"Is your son home?"

"Probably. If he is, he's still asleep. He didn't get home until five in the morning, the hooligan!"

Frantisek Novak was indeed still asleep. The chairman was about to awaken him violently but the lieutenant held him back.

"Wait a minute!"

A kit bag belonging to the young wanderer was lying on the floor by the bed. The lieutenant reached into it, rummaged about, and pulled his hand out. In his palm he held a heavy nine-millimeter German pistol, a Parabellum. He removed the magazine. It contained only two rounds; he knew it could hold considerably more than that. He peered down the barrel. In the darkness he could see a coppery glint, the rounded head of a bullet. The lieutenant sniffed at the barrel and then gave it to the chairman to sniff as well.

"That little bastard!"

The violent awakening proceeded, and the lieutenant made no attempt to intervene.

. . .

"I'm telling you, I don't *know* her name!" the wanderer swore, rubbing his eyes. A dark blue bruise was rapidly forming around one of them. "She calls herself Marylou. I never asked her what her second name was. She works at Tesla, on the television line. And I only used the pistol to shoot at pine cones. Okay, so I was showing off. I know it's dumb. What's the big deal? Tell me something that *isn't* dumb! But I sure never killed anybody."

"We'll see about that," said Lieutenant Boruvka. He left the pale chairman, and escorted his delinquent back to Prague.

. . .

In a huge hall a swarm of girls were sitting beside a jerky assembly-line belt, glancing curiously at the plump lieutenant, the black-haired Malek (who had sucked in his stomach and thrust out his chest), and the kid with the black eye. Escorted by both policemen and the workshop foreman, the kid was walking slowly along the line, looking the girls over. When he got to the end he said, "She's not here. But I'm not bullshitting. She said she worked here on the television line."

"So your alibi is up the spout, smartass!" said Malek.

"Maybe she's on the rag and didn't come."

"Oh, she's suddenly on the rag!" said Malek. "And when was the last time you slept together?"

"So she screwed off for the day—how should I know? I only know she told me she worked on the TV assembly line at Tesla. This here's the Tesla plant, this here's the assembly line, and there's the TV sets."

The lieutenant turned to the foreman. "Is anyone missing?"

"Someone may have stepped out," said the foreman, looking around. "There's a substitute in number seven's place."

"So one of them is—"

"In the can," said the foreman.

Just then the door of the women's toilet opened and out walked a peroxide blonde. When she saw the kid with the black eye she said, "Hey, hi there!"

"Hi," said the kid. And he had his alibi.

. . .

Sergeant Malek was annoyed. He was even more annoyed when Jandacek, the ballistics expert, reported that although the kid's pistol had been fired recently, its bullets didn't have anything like the rifling marks on the bullets that had killed the girls. He also reported that the three submachine guns collected from Hemele, Ruzicka, and Koubek had to be excluded as murder weapons as well.

The lieutenant hardly listened to the ballistics expert's report. He was—absent-mindedly, it seemed—drawing something like a map on a piece of paper. The sergeant looked over his shoulder at the drawing:

"What's that for, Josef?" he asked.

"I don't know," said the lieutenant truthfully. "I think we'll go back to Ouhlice."

. . .

Lieutenant Silny, the duty officer, was sitting almost at attention opposite the detective in the Cultural Room. On the wall was a portrait of the new first secretary, saved by the exodus of the flat steel monsters they had witnesssed last night.

"I set out with my platoon in the armored personnel carrier at 0812, according to orders," declared the officer. "At 0820 hours I crossed the bridge over the Uplava and at 0830, in the U1 woods, we came up against an unforeseen impediment to our progress. I had to suspend the original order and request an update."

He recounted everything with absolute certainty, and with far more ease than he'd displayed the day before, when he'd told the story about the breakdown—something he had obviously concocted on the spot. Either he'd forgotten his original story or he had since consulted someone about the matter. Lieutenant Silny was clearly an exemplary officer. He was wearing a sharpshooter's badge, the badge of Political Maturity, and the badge of Physical Prowess. Only his unusually small cranium suggested that the officer's intelligence might not be sufficient for a badge, much less a medal.

"Couldn't you simply have driven around this—this unforeseen impediment?" asked the detective. "Isn't the troop carrier an all-terrain vehicle?"

"The terrain on both sides of the U1 woods is too rough to be passable for our vehicles," said the officer. "We'd have had to go back to Okrouhlice and take a detour along a route that goes through Prastvi, Ledec, Kostelovice, Zivny, Konin—and over the summit of Hratvi. A total of one hundred and seven kilometers."

"I see," said the lieutenant. "So you were waiting for your orders to be updated, and you were still waiting when we arrived at the scene of the crime."

"Affirmitive."

"How do you explain the delay?"

"Major Kadavy never explained it to me," said the officer reluctantly. "I suppose he—he had to get an authorization from—from the division commander, General Svlacec."

"Hmmm," said the old detective, wondering what kind of an officer this was if, despite his badges of merit, he required such a precise set of authorizations. When he had been doing his own stint in the army, the officers had been—but then he remembered Lieutenant Hezky and how once, during maneuvers, he had shifted his entire tank platoon to elevation point 606—precisely according to orders—to pick up a reserve supply of ammunition. Instead of ammunition, however, they had run into the enemy's main command post. The entire platoon had been captured, along with the lieutenant. It turned out that while he was navigating from the turret of the lead tank, Lieutenant Hezky had accidentally turned the map upside down; instead of leading his unit to elevation point 606, he had taken them to elevation point 909. How he had managed to follow the route on an upside-down map remained one of the best-kept military secrets.

"Hmmm," repeated the lieutenant. "And when did the new orders actually arrive?"

"At 1617."

"And what were the orders?"

"To return to the barracks in Okrouhlice."

"Can you tell me more about this—unexpected impediment?"

For a long time the officer did not answer. Then he said slowly, "I'd have to get special permission from Comrade Major Kadavy—or maybe from Comrade General Svlacec."

. . .

"I think we should have another chat with those three soldiers," the lieutenant decided. But Sergeant Malek protested.

"They've told us all they know, Josef. We'd be better off asking the major. Or, better still, going straight to the general. Why go to the blacksmith when—"

"I wouldn't like to bother them," objected the lieutenant. "I expect they've got problems enough of their own right now."

"Don't be such a softie, Josef." The sergeant thought for a moment, then went on. "Look here: an unforeseen impediment, and they had to go all the way up to the general to deal with it. Wouldn't we be better off passing the ball to the general and then spending our time with the draftees who dated those smartass girls?" What he said seemed a sudden contradiction to his original reluctance to question the first three witnesses again.

"I have a feeling the unforeseen impediment is somehow connected with all of this," the lieutenant told him.

"That's just what I mean! I feel exactly the same way! So we're better off playing dumb and interrogating witnesses we won't get any more out of anyway. That's by far the best way, Josef, believe me. I got a nose for these things. A political nose."

· · ·

In the end the lieutenant compromised, as he had done several times recently. He sent Malek to Oresi to ask the sister of the murdered girl whether the intelligent Jarmila had rejected any other suitors besides Franta. He himself went to take a look around the U1 woods.

The woods smelled of pine pitch, and green dragonflies were darting back and forth across the road. The lieutenant could hear a cuckoo calling and from somewhere in the cool shade there came the tapping of a woodpecker. He stopped. On a branch arching out over the road, a black squirrel had interrupted its work and was sitting motionless with a pine cone in its mouth, watching the intruder. As the branch swayed in the mild June breeze, the squirrel sat there like a dark, motionless goblin, a mesmerizing little imp.

The lieutenant stepped off the road, waded through a patch of ferns, and found himself in a clearing. On the grass in the middle of the clearing there was a dry patch of oil.

He looked around. Tall spruce trees were waving gently against a background of blue dotted with small white clouds. Far above the clouds, he could see a four-engine jet moving slowly across the sky.

He walked across the clearing and looked through the bushes. Beyond the woods a gentle, grassy slope rose to the place where the terrain became rough and impassable even for tracked vehicles. The grass was fresh and green. It was there in that grass, at the edge of the woods, that the two girls had lain yesterday, their bodies composing a pretty, seemingly prearranged picture in the grass.

The lieutenant turned around and retreated to the woods.

• • •

He could hear flies buzzing in the warm June sun. He looked around. The mossy ground among the trees bore traces of recent human activities. A broken tin spoon shone dimly from a bed of moss that had been torn, it seemed, by heavy boots. On a stump somebody had extinguished the butt of a filterless cigarette. A leather strap with a cracked buckle was half hidden under a blueberry bush with no berries left on its tiny branches. Next to it was a ball of crumpled newspaper.

The lieutenant picked it up and smoothed it out on the stump, removing the butt and putting it in his pocket. There were bold headlines on the front page but he couldn't read them; they were in an alphabet he had never learned. He hadn't needed it in criminal investigation—though it would have been useful in the *other* police force.

• • •

Half an hour later he was in the barracks in Ouhlice. He asked for Corporal Hemele and took him for a drive in the squad car. They drove down to the river in silence and crossed the bridge. When they reached the woods, the lieutenant pulled over onto the shoulder and stopped.

"Why did you go into the woods on Sunday morning, corporal?"

"To pick blueberries."

"You told me you went to have a sleep."

"There was that too. First to eat and then to sleep."

The lieutenant listened to the sounds of the woods, peered into the green shade, and remembered what this young man and his friends had told him about those two funny girls. What had happened was now clear. A dark shadow fell across the lieutenant's soul.

"It's very commendable of you, not wanting to reveal something your commanding officer told you was a military secret," said the lieutenant. "But you needn't feel bound by that. I know why you were given some free time. I know what that unforeseen obstruction was, and I know why Lieutenant Silny had to go back to the major and then all the way up to the general for a change in orders. And because I know that, I also know," he said, looking straight at the young man sitting beside him, "that you didn't go into the woods for blueberries, and you didn't go into the woods for a nap."

"You know?" The corporal was clearly relieved.

"It would interest me to know what happened in the woods."

"Nothing," said the corporal. "You can't talk to them. We just wanted to shoot the breeze with them, but they're scared shitless of their officers." The corporal became excited. "We wanted to explain that we don't need them here, that we can handle things ourselves and the longer they stay here, the more people will get pissed off at them, and in the end everyone will get hurt."

"Did you tell them all that?"

"We started to. Just a bit past the edge of the woods, we came across a sentry. They were spread out, not just on the road where we first came across them when we tried to drive through on the troop carrier. They were all over the place, in the woods—packing up in a hurry, it seemed to me. It was a mapping unit. Over there on that rock—" he pointed to a tall, massive outcropping that rose above the tops of the fir trees "they had a camera with a big telephoto lens, and they were just dismantling it."

"And you talked with the sentry?"

"We did and we didn't. As soon as he eyeballed us he pointed his gun at us and said, 'Halt or I'll shoot!' In Russian, of course. Jindra Ruzicka, the lance-corporal—you've already talked to him—"

The lieutenant nodded.

"He knows Russian pretty good, his mother's Russian, and he says, 'Don't be crazy, man! We're in the Warsaw Pact too, and besides that, we're brothers, like, we're all Slavs, right?' But old Vasiliev there, he was quivering in his boots, scared to death, and he points that submachine at us and says, 'Halt or I'll shoot!' again, so we halt—" As the lieutenant listened to him he saw the scene in his mind: the terrified soldier on sentry duty in a foreign country while his superior officers photographed the terrain of the foreign country through a telephoto lens; a soldier with his head shaved, but lacking the relaxed tradition of the Good Soldier Svejk, whose head was also shaved. "And Jindra says, 'Come off it, you jerk! We just want to tell you that we'd all be better off if you'd—' " And the lieutenant saw those two suntanned girls in their summery blouses and miniskirts, emerging from the bushes to collect their ludicrous luxury tax on a recruit's horniness. But this time they weren't out to collect their tax. This time they wanted—"So Vasiliev there cocks his weapon and he's practically shouting. I tell you, comrade lieutenant, he was hysterical—" The girls probably wanted to say the same things the corporal and his fellow soldiers wanted to say, but they had no experience with soldiers. Or rather, they had—but with soldiers of a completely different kind. They didn't, or couldn't, take the situation seriously. A moonlit Bohemian night, two seventeen-year-old girls, a Russian soldier with his head shaved bare. Of course, regulations are regulations, but they're there to be broken, not to be taken literally; at least, that was how the girls saw it, that was what experience had taught them. The lieutenant could almost hear the teasing voice of the one who'd wanted to be a doctor. "I tell you," the voice of the corporal insisted, "I thought he really meant it seriously. And he did, the idiot! *Halt! I'm going to shoot!* I look at his face, comrade lieutenant, and I see he's scared shitless of getting into trouble, so I say, 'Let's get the hell out of here, there's no sense in trying to talk to him. He hasn't got a mind of his own.' So we turned around and walked back."

But the girls had not turned back. In their world, in their tradition, it was unimaginable that a soldier would really obey standing orders like that to the letter. After all, another soldier in a similar situation had said, "Hey, hold on there, what's your name?" And when they had told him he had said, "Hey, don't be crazy. If they catch you here you're going to be in real trouble."

But this soldier didn't say that. He repeated this idiotic warning three times, as the regulations required, and then—terrified of what his officers might do if he disobeyed—he opened fire. A modern submachine gun fires so rapidly that it's a small matter to place four bullets in a neat row in a single body before that body slumps to the ground, and three into a second body before the person realizes what's happening and turns around to run.

It suddenly occurred to the lieutenant that his entire investigation had been pointless. Up there, in the regions of command known as "upstairs," they knew who the murderer was. He wondered for a moment how they would justify taking him off the case this time, when he hadn't committed the slightest act of insubordination.

· · ·

They took him off the case with no justification whatsoever. And he—he did not demand any. He felt helpless. One night about two months after the unsolved case of the double murder in the grass—no solution was ever announced—he stood at the open window of his sitting room; it was past midnight and the half-empty bottle of slivovitz (hidden from Mrs. Boruvka) had put him in a desperate mood. It was a starry night, the tile roofs shone a brilliant vermilion, and black shadows of cats could be seen flitting across them. It was the time of rutting, the time for the St. Wenceslas kittens to be conceived.

From somewhere in the darkness he could hear a rumbling, strangely metallic sound. A dark, regular throbbing of heavy vehicles moving slowly through the streets. He raised his eyes to the stars. Large, black shadows were approaching across the sky. He had never seen such heavy air traffic after midnight.

It was those distant shadows—not the detective—that finally settled the case of the ornament in the grass.

Humbug

The lieutenant earnestly hoped that his daughter's affair with the American would soon culminate in a wedding, and he had good grounds for such hope. But then Mack had an accident that excluded him from normal life for fourteen months, and the affair dragged on for another two years. What happened was that Mack got in the way of a bullet fired from a machine gun mounted on a tank. He was fortunate the bullet only damaged his thighbone, for another shot from the same gun in the same general direction struck one of his fellow students in the head as she was holding up a picture of First Secretary Dubcek for the benefit of the soldiers on the tanks. At least she was spared a lot of unpleasantness at school; the cadre personnel in charge of establishing each student's political behavior during the days of brotherly help did not bother with the childless dead. Mack himself did have difficulties, but his professor, a specialist in mesozoic turtles, displayed almost superhuman heroism and a keen understanding of political tactics. With the help of a statement Mack's father had once made to the press to get out of military service in Korea, the professor managed to persuade the cadre people not to expel the wounded foreign student from the Department of Palaeontology.

. . .

Lieutenant Boruvka survived all the upsets and reversals of that unsettled time after the Soviet invasion with his credentials intact. But his conscience, which gnawed at him during the best of times, was transformed into a toothy, piscatory fossil that his future son-in-law compared to those fish in the Paraná River that are capable of rapidly stripping the flesh off anyone unfortunate enough to fall in. The lieutenant, crushed by the events and once more mindful of his family's welfare, filled out the required questionnaires almost truthfully—except for the section labeled *Origin,* where he neglected to mention (as his father had neglected to mention in 1939, after a somewhat similar invasion) the fact that his otherwise demonstrably Catholic great-grandmother had had the suspicious maiden name of Silberstein. Guided by hints from politically adaptable colleagues, and using the language of the leading daily newspaper, he confessed that at the time of the Entry of the Fraternal Armies (this was what the press was now calling the invasion) he had been misled by revisionist propaganda and had succumbed to an emotional attitude to the events, but that he had been assailed by growing doubts until finally he had thrown off his emotional attitude and fully identified with the politics of the Party and the government. Sergeant Malek manufactured a model reply upon these lines for the entire Criminal Investigation Division, and all the officers used it on their questionnaires and ratified their admissions of error with their own signatures.

Thus the lieutenant navigated safely through dangerous waters—at the minor expense of a perjured declaration—and they even promoted him to first lieutenant for good behavior. Malek was made a lieutenant and the two filled out new questionnaires concerning their opinions on Vietnam, Korea, and the first and second world wars (all of them bourgeois-imperialist conflicts except for the Great Patriotic War of Russia against Hitlerite Germany), the Arab-Israeli conflict (Zionist aggression), Franz Kafka (totally alien to the socialist reader), Mao Tse Tung (head of the Chinese revisionist clique), pacifism (cosmopolitan idealistic trick to weaken the Peace Camp of Socialism), the assassination of Reinhard Heydrich (the politically irresponsible act of traitorous bourgeois émigrés), and many other items of ideological importance.

To the lieutenant's surprise, Major Kautsky, the division's former head, turned out to be a diehard revisionist. Instead of using Malek's model answer on his questionnaire he wrote, in the language of the leading newspaper, that he did not agree with the Entry of the Fraternal Armies. To make matters worse, he continued his hostile fraternization with the Dubcekist former minister of the Interior, Pavel, who had fought in Spain. In addition he formed a friendship with an expelled member of the Central Committee of the Party, Kriegl—who was a Jew, refused to sign the Moscow agreement about the temporary stationing of the Russian army on Czechoslovak territory, and as a young man had fought with Mao Tse Tung in China. Finally, along with his son and daughter, Major Kautsky was arrested for distributing leaflets reminding people of their constitutional right not to vote in the forthcoming elections (the government nevertheless received a mandate of 99.99 ½ percent).

The division gained a new chief, Major Tlama, and a new sergeant, Vladimir Pudil.

. . .

The first case that gave the lieutenant an opportunity to appreciate the expertise of his new subordinate officer was the murder of Ondrej Krasa, who drove a delivery truck for the Candy and Sweets Communal Enterprises. Krasa's body was found by a pair of lovers in a Prague park. It was lying on a pathway beneath a blood-red moon. He had a fractured skull; someone had struck him from behind, probably with a heavy tool like a hammer or a wrench. He was still fairly young, thirty-five according to his ID booklet. Sergeant Pudil, the new acquisition of the Homicide Division and chairman of the criminal division's Soviet Socialist Youth, called the Ministry of the Interior from a phone booth in the park. A

firm suspicion had formed in his mind that there was a class motivation for the crime since the murdered man not only was a worker,
according to his ID booklet, but had a letter in his pocket revealing that he had recently been given a bonus for exemplary work.
To be completely certain, Pudil wanted the dead man's political
profile.

In all his years of service Lieutenant Boruvka had never once
resorted to Secret Police files for information, and when they got
back to the division he looked into the criminal records. With a
feeling of satisfaction (of which he immediately felt ashamed, for
it was a malicious feeling) he informed his new sergeant that the
exemplary worker had had a criminal record. Krasa had once studied
economics, but in 1965 he had been arrested for failing to report
a crime—intent to leave the country without permission—and had
been sentenced to six years in prison. The married couple who
had tried unsuccessfully to escape had panicked and told police
things they might have kept silent about with impunity, and so it
came out that Ondrej Krasa had originally intended to go with
them. In the end he hadn't because his girlfriend, Lida Oharikova,
who was not yet seventeen at the time, didn't want to leave her
widowed mother behind alone. Krasa denied (rather illogically)
that Oharikova knew anything about the intended crime and told
the court he had decided not to go because he couldn't bring
himself to part with his young girlfriend. Eventually the public
prosecutor decided not to press charges against Oharikova, but
he made a great deal of some other circumstances revealed by the
terrified couple. Krasa, they confessed, had provided them with a
military map of the border region in the Sumava forest; he had
stolen the map during army maneuvers in the region, and the
public prosecutor characterized this as a betrayal of military secrets.
He asked that Krasna be given six years and the judge brought
his gavel down on it.

Krasa dutifully served his time. His girlfriend got married four
years after his arrest, and as soon as he got out Krasa married
someone else, but within a year they were divorced. When Ser-

geant Pudil came to Boruvka with his report, the lieutenant could
not resist being sarcastic. "You needn't have bothered the comrades, comrade. I don't suppose they told you we have something
called criminal records right here in the division."

But Pudil had some surprising information which the criminal
records had not yielded.

"They did tell me, comrade lieutenant. But our records aren't
as complete as the ones they have at Interior. Did you know, for
example, that Krasa was a Zionist?"

"No, I didn't. Why would someone called Krasa—"

"Because his name isn't Krasa, that's why. It's Schoenfeld. You
see how unreliable our records are, leaving out important information like that? And in 1968 Schoenfeld had a meeting with
someone called Cohen," said the sergeant, pronouncing the name
phonetically as *Tsohen*, "in the lobby of the Alcron Hotel. And
this Cohen," he declared importantly, "is a member of the Zionist
organization American Express Inc.—and what's more, his name
isn't Cohen at all, it's Kohn. What do you think of that, comrade?"

"Cohen is the American form of our Kohn," said the lieutenant
drily. That much he knew from his future son-in-law.

"That's beside the point," the sergeant shot back. "The important thing is that it's an alias. The two of them got together in the
Terezin ghetto when they were kids, and Cohen is in fact from
Breclav. Are you aware, comrade, of what a perfect combination
that is for subversive activity? Since we're not equipped to handle
stuff like this in Homicide, I recommend that we investigate only
the basic facts and then turn the whole thing over, lock, stock,
and barrel, to the comrades in Counter-Espionage."

Silence followed. Malek looked uncertainly at his superior officer. Recently, Boruvka felt, Malek had somehow lost his former
impetuosity and élan; despite his promotion he was now display-
ing a respect for the new sergeant that belied the differences in
their ranks and professional qualifications. So he replied, "Our job
is to track down the murderer. What the comrades in Interior do

with the culprit is, shall we say, their own business—perhaps. It's not our job to pass judgment on what is or is not our political jurisdiction. In every murder case we have full authority to ensure that justice takes its course."

"On the one hand you're quite right, comrade," said Pudil. "But on the other hand, everything has to be approached from the political angle—especially now, when the main task our society faces is to eliminate political deformations caused by Dubcek and his revisionist clique."

.   .   .

And indeed the Party and the government, along with unde-formed citizens, were hard at work, vigilantly eliminating deformations—as the lieutenant discovered for himself that very evening.

Coming home after a full day of investigation, he found himself in a vale of tears. Mrs. Boruvka was lying on the couch with a cold compress on her forehead. In place of their usual coal-black outlines, Zuzana's eyes were rimmed with a red that that was entirely natural. Mack was gloomily pacing up and down, strumming his guitar, but he stopped when the lieutenant stepped into the room. Mr. and Mrs. McLaughlin were sitting at the kitchen table. The lieutenant's heart stopped beating for a moment. He was anticipating the worst.

"They've banished us from the republic," declared Mr. McLaughlin in a sepulchral voice. "For serving as English announcers on those radio stations that went underground during the Soviet invasion."

The lieutenant had been afraid this would come back to haunt them one day. Mr. McLaughlin's voice, heavy with the unmistakable accent of his native Tennessee, had been recorded not only by monitors in the West but also by the pro-Soviet radio stations located in East Germany at the time, though pretending to broadcast from "somewhere in Bohemia." But two years had gone by, Mr. McLaughlin was still playing trumpet in the Lucerna Bar, and Lieutenant Boruvka had begun to hope that the whole thing might have been forgotten in high places.

"They gave us twenty-four hours," said Mr. McLaughlin, "and when I asked whether Mack could remain behind because he wants to marry a Czech girl—"

Wants to marry. . . . The lieutenant hardly expected that his innermost hopes concerning Mack and his daughter would be fulfilled under such bad, if not tragic, circumstances. But in spite of the circumstances, a wave of warmth filled his paternal heart. Then he realized that his future brother-in-law was addressing a question to him:

"When I asked, do you know what that weasel of a policeman said?"

The lieutenant shook his head but a dark premonition began to overshadow the warm feeling in his heart.

"He said, 'We don't believe in breaking up families,' " Mack interjected bitterly. "So I'm getting turfed out with my parents. And the cop told me that even if I did marry Zuzana, I couldn't expect to get permission to stay."

The lieutenant stopped feeling well, but he overcame the pain that now gripped his heart and said bravely, "Well then, I suppose Zuzana will have to go to America with you. We'll miss her but—but—a woman's place is with her husband."

"Guess again, Father," Zuzana interrupted. "The cop also told Mack that just because he's going to marry me he shouldn't expect they'll let me go with him, because I've got Lucy and Mack's not her father."

"He said what?" shouted the lieutenant, and the blood rose to his head. "That—that—"

"We'll get married first thing in the morning," said Mack. "And we'll think of something. Maybe I could get my cousin Laureen in Memphis to help. She'd come here, you could paste Zuzana's picture in her passport— "the lieutenant leaped for the telephone and took it off the hook"—Zuzana could fly out, Laureen could claim she'd lost her passport, and the American embassy would give her a new one. She's an American citizen, so they can't do anything to her." The lieutenant had the receiver up to his ear but he could hear nothing, and he hoped that no one else could either.

He watched his daughter trying valiantly to hold back her tears, and succumbed to one of his many fits of paternal love. Then he got his feelings under control again and began unscrewing the receiver, just to make sure.

"You'll get married, no question," he said decisively, "but forget about that idea with your cousin, Mack. You're still young and you can stick it out for a year or two. Meanwhile I'll do what I can."

He realized what this could mean for a man in his position, what secret obligations he might be exposed to. Even blackmail. But he also knew that he would go through anything for Zuzana and Mack, even if those little fish picked the last ounce of flesh from his bones. "Things will have to ease up here again," he said uncertainly, and then added, "and I think that right now a lot of people can be—ahem—" turning to the telephone, he unscrewed the mouthpiece and disconnected the bell "—bribed. I'll find a way, don't worry."

"But what if they won't let me out even then, Mack?" said Zuzana desperately. "You're not going to—you can't always—"

"I'll get you out of here," said Mack resolutely.

"But I don't want you to feel—just because of those idiots—" Zuzana swallowed the terrible word. "I'll marry you, Mack—" and the lieutenant saw that the natural pluck of his athletic daughter was rapidly fading "—but if they still haven't let me go after two—" and she stopped and sobbed "—or five years at the most, then promise—promise me you'll get a divorce—" The pivotwoman who had once made the national basketball team as a spare collapsed on the table and began to weep uncontrollably.

The lieutenant clenched his fists. Suddenly he was overcome by a feeling he had never known before. It wasn't just hatred. It was beyond that. It was a kind of feeling he had only heard about—in political courses. Could this, he caught himself wondering, be class hatred?

· · ·

There was nothing either glorious or gay about the wedding, but it was fast and, because several officials had to be bribed (the normal waiting period was three months), it was expensive as well. The only thing suggesting a traditional wedding was the bridesmaid, who wore white. Four-year-old Lucy had, with great weeping, refused to give up her promised function, even in these exceptional circumstances, and so behind Mack in his Sunday best and Zuzana in her suit for the theater stood a little girl in a white lace dress. Instead of the promised train she held a piece of pink ribbon which they had fastened, for that purpose, around the bride's waist. It was a civil ceremony, and in promising to honor and obey the republic and its socialist system the newlyweds may well have sworn a false oath. Indeed, Mack, with his pending expulsion, was committing what amounted to perjury. The lieutenant's mind was so distracted by the multiple ironies of the ceremony that he forgot to tip the officiator; although the man had already been abundantly bribed, habit got the better of him and he deliberately burned a hole in the marriage certificate with his cigarette.

The McLaughlins almost missed the Pan American flight out of Prague. Barely an hour after the wedding the bride was standing on the windswept observation deck, deafened by the roar of four jet engines and watching the plane carry her husband into the leaden clouds hanging low over the airport. Driving home in a taxi, the lieutenant was overwhelmed by a hatred he now definitely identified as the feeling described in textbooks on Marxism-Leninism—a feeling he had once regarded as purely theoretical.

. . .

The essential facts of the murder—the only ones Sergeant Pudil was prepared to go into before handing the case over to the more appropriate police force—were easy enough to ascertain. Not long before he was found dead on the pathway of the Nusle Gardens by the lovers, Ondrej Krasa had been drinking beer in the Mermaid Tavern in Podoli with two of his co-workers, Svata Kudelka and Jindra Nebesky. According to the testimony of his pals, he had made a telephone call just before setting out on his fateful journey home. Neither Kudelka nor Nebesky knew whom he had talked to.

The lieutenant's group of detectives questioned Krasa's co-workers in the garage belonging to the Candy and Sweets Communal Enterprises, but Sergeant Pudil played first violin all the way. Boruvka realized that he had somehow lost interest in his work, and even Malek was more reticent than usual. But the chairman of the Soviet Socialist Youth (known popularly as the SS Youth) completely made up for their lack of zeal.

"What kind of man was this Schoenfeld, comrades?" he asked the circle of drivers sitting on the workbenches or leaning against the walls of the garage.

After a long pause, Jindra Nebesky said, "Schoenfeld?"

"You didn't know his real name was Schoenfeld?" asked the sergeant in mock surprise. "I suppose that's natural. He'd have kept it a secret. I'm talking about Krasa."

"Oh, him. A great guy," said Nebesky with feeling.

"That's a fact," said another driver with a shock of blond hair. "Never a party-pooper. Always stuck by the group."

"Did you know he'd been in jail for a political crime?"

"Oh, that. Sure, I knew he'd done something dumb once," admitted Nebesky.

"But he was only twenty when he did it. Not even that—nineteen at the most," interjected a driver with a classic Czech button nose. His name was Cespiva. "And he did it for his friends. That's an extenuating circumstance."

"There are no circumstances in the world," Pudil reminded him severely, "that can extenuate betraying the republic."

"But he did his time," said Svata Kudelka, who was also a driver. "And for as long as he was with us, he worked like the devil. Just ask the boss."

"That doesn't surprise me. Elements like him are good at masking their true feelings. Did he have any contact with other Zionists?"

The drivers looked at each other uncomfortably.

"As far as I know, anyway, there aren't any of that sort around here," said Cespiva.

"What about the assistant manager?" asked Pudil triumphantly. "Comrade Roth? He certainly wasn't buddies with Krasa." Cespiva shook his head. "And besides, Comrade Roth is not a—what d'you call them—Zionist. He's a Communist. Chairman of the Party organization. As far as we know, Ondra only hung around with us. Ever since he got divorced he was kind of a loner. But, like I say, he was a great guy."

"Did any foreigners ever come to see him?"

Once more the drivers looked at each other. Then Kudelka said, "Never heard of any foreigners. Do you guys know of any foreigners?"

All the drivers shook their heads in unison. It occurred to the lieutenant that their collective evidence was adding up to the portrait of a quasi-saint. Perhaps these simple men were keeping silent about something—not Pudil's fantastic connections, which, the old detective's experience told him, were unlikely to exist outside the political pages of the Party daily—but something that might have blemished Krasa's image. After all, people have some deep-rooted taboos, one of which is against speaking ill of the dead. The lieutenant himself honored such traditions. But only off duty.

Malek may possibly have been thinking along the same lines, for he plucked up his courage and said, "You guys are making him out to be some kind of angel. Didn't he even pick his nose?"

The group of drivers again exchanged uneasy glances. Then Cespiva spoke. "I'm telling you, comrade, he was a great guy, honest. Except for beer he never drank, and he didn't even smoke."

"I'll bet he wore a halo too, eh?"

"Pretty near," retorted Cespiva. "He only had one weakness and he couldn't help that."

"Women?"

"A woman. One woman," said Cespiva. "The bitch who couldn't wait for him to get out. Lida Oharikova. She was the reason his marriage bust up too."

"And anyways, he only married someone else because he was pissed off at her," said Kudelka. "At least, that's what he said."

"Aha," said Malek. "So he picked up where he'd left off six years before?"

Once more the drivers paused for a moment of silent consultation. Then Nebesky spoke. "No sense in trying to hush it up. You'll find out anyway," he said. "He was seeing her. And once he told Svata here that he was going to marry her one day, and that she was hardly sleeping with her old man any more, anyway."

"Enough of this false solidarity, comrades!" Pudil piped up. "What about foreign women?"

"We'll look into that later," the lieutenant interrupted quickly. They were the only words he had uttered during the entire interrogation.

.   .   .

An hour later he was looking at the walls of a room in a co-op flat. They were hung with paintings depicting a variety of setting suns, Prague's skyline with Hradcany Castle, and cows grazing against a background of white birch. He looked at the cheap furniture of no definable style, and at the young woman in a duster, whose eyes were large, black, and—as Zuzana's had been not long ago—ringed with red circles.

"I did wait for him. Almost five years. But you know, I was very young and silly. I'll never forgive myself as long as I live. Any woman would count herself lucky if she had a man like—like Ondra."

"I understand. Your husband's a metalworker, is that right?" asked Malek.

"Yes. In the CKD plant."

"That him?" Malek pointed to a photograph of a mustached muscleman in a wrestler's leotard covered with more medals than the average Soviet general.

"Yes, that's Sucharipa. Franta. He's on the Hercules team in Nusle."

Malek looked significantly at the lieutenant, but when he found no sign of comprehension he turned towards Pudil. The sergeant, however, was studying the young woman's physiognomy closely.

She had black hair, black eyes, a rather large and somewhat angular nose, and full red lips. The sergeant, unaware that Malek was looking at him, asked with characteristic directness, "What are your origins, comrade?"

She looked startled. "Working class," she said, "except one grandfather who was a private cobbler. But he employed only members of his own family."

"That's not what I mean. I was thinking of your—"

"You were saying," the lieutenant broke in, "that Mr. Kraska was a good man and that you regret not having waited for him. It is possible that recently you may have come to some kind of an—ah—understanding?"

The young woman turned pink. The lieutenant could tell a good deal from the expression of her eyes. He knew very well that the sergeant suspected her of having origins he would refer to as "racial"—but the sergeant was unaware of the connotations that word had for the lieutenant, who, twice already in his lifetime, had had to keep silent about the maiden name of one of his grandmothers. But, the old detective thought, perhaps he just doesn't know any better—he was born after the war. Still, they shouldn't—

"We've ascertained," he said quietly, "that you were seeing Mr. Krasa. Is that how it was?"

The woman looked at him. She was the color of a peony.

"Yes. I wanted a divorce. We met every Wednesday. I usually go to see my mother that day, so my husband never suspected—at least—" She stopped.

"Well, did he or didn't he?" asked Malek sharply.

"I mean he didn't know we were meeting on Wednesdays because Mother covered up for us. She's never liked Franta, she says he's a crude bully. She says all wrestlers are bullies."

"And is he?" asked Malek.

The black eyes looked down.

"Has he ever beaten you?"

The woman nodded. "Someone told him about Ondra and me. An anonymous phone call. So Franta wanted me to tell him if it was true or not."

She was silent again. Malek said, "And he beat you, is that it?" The woman lifted her eyes and looked at the lieutenant. "Yes. But I told him straight to his face that I was going to divorce him and marry Ondra. And then he went out looking for Ondra—"

"So he roughed up your sweetheart too, is that it?" asked Malek.

Unexpectedly, the woman answered with a tone of pride in her voice.

"Not at all. Ondra beat *him* up. Sucharipa had to go to the hospital and they gave him seven stitches, here." She pointed to her forehead.

Malek looked at Pudil, but the SS Youth chairman was still scrutinizing the woman's suspicious-looking nose from behind half-closed blond eyelashes. So Malek turned to the lieutenant and whistled softly. This time the lieutenant reacted. "But you said your husband was a wrestler."

"He's a heavyweight, but I don't know if you could really call him a wrestler. He usually just stands with his feet planted apart; his opponents pull and push, but he weighs 148 kilos and they never manage to budge him. Most of his matches end in a draw. That's why they keep him on at the club—he guarantees them at least a point in any competition. Once in a blue moon the other fellow loses his balance and Franta falls on him and pins him for two points." She spoke with deep disgust. "But basically he's a clumsy coward. And Ondra knew how to box. Before they locked—before he was sentenced, he boxed in tournaments. First he closed Franta's eyes so badly they swelled up like onions. And then, because Ondra was wearing a kind of—well, a kind of ring—"

"Was that from you?" Malek interrupted.

"Well—yes, from me. Anyway, then Ondra knocked him out—he hit him on the head so hard they had to put seven stitches into him," said the wrestler's wife, almost proudly.

. . .

"Obvious, isn't it?" deduced Malek when they were back in the car. "A wrestler, 148 kilos. Krasa was a shrimp, weighed only 67 kilos when he died, and he knocks him out and gives him an inferiority complex. And on top of that he's crawling into bed with the guy's old lady. According to the coroner's report, Krasa was killed with a blunt instrument, probably a hammer or wrench. So there you are—let's go wrap him up."

The lieutenant nodded gloomily, but before he could say anything the sergeant spoke up. "Did you look at that woman? A hook nose, dark as a crow, Hapsburg lips, a narrow face—"

"So what?" asked Malek uneasily.

"And Krasa was a boxer!" The sergeant raised his eyebrows dramatically. "Have you ever heard of a boxer punching someone in the forehead?"

"It wasn't exactly a regulation match."

"It makes no sense for a boxer to hit anyone in the forehead. But *they* train them that way," said Pudil mysteriously. "In karate. See what I'm getting at? It's a kind of South Korean fighting technique used for killing your opponent."

"In the West, maybe," said the lieutenant. "But Krasa was never in the West."

"Ah, but he was," said the sergeant triumphantly. "Right after the entry of the fraternal armies. Schoenfeld spent a week in Vienna."

The lieutenant couldn't resist loading his response with irony. "A week? And they taught him karate? Is that what you're saying?"

"A crash course," said the sergeant eagerly—himself a product of a crash course in criminology. "They have their methods."

"I doubt it," said the lieutenant. Although Pudil should have praised Boruvka's skeptical assessment of Western spy centers, he argued.

"I wouldn't underestimate them, comrade. Zionist circles have been stepping up their efforts recently. Look at how they're stirring up trouble in the Soviet Union: they all want to emigrate to Israel, which is out-and-out provocation. We weren't born yesterday."

"Well, that's very—interesting," said Malek, "but I don't see what it has to do with—"

"They're so goddamn full of themselves!" shouted the SS chairman, beginning to lose his temper. "They want to turn the wheel of history back! They call themselves the chosen people! But the historical role of the working class—"

. . .

All the way to the CKD factory to see the 148-kilo giant, Pudil tried to enlighten his superior officers on the Zionist conspiracy against peace, about which they displayed miserably little knowledge. When they found Sucharipa in the plant, the sergeant regarded him with undisguised sympathy. Also, he was working on the low turret of a tank into which some others were installing a naval cannon, and this sent Pudil into such transports of enthusiasm that he let Boruvka ask all the questions.

"That wasn't fair," said the giant, pointing to a flaming red scar on his forehead. "I'll bet he was wearing a set of knucks."

"Apparently he closed both your eyes," said the lieutenant. "Was that with brass knuckles too?"

"That wasn't fair either. A boxer always has the advantage over a Graeco-Roman wrestler, and he fought dirty. He landed a one-two punch to my brows and blew out both my lights and then, when I couldn't see for the blood, that's when he probably slipped on the knucks."

"And you haven't seen him since he assaulted you, comrade?" asked the sergeant at last, having managed to overcome his fascination with the flattened gun turret.

"No. But he had the nerve to call me."

"When was that?" asked the detective.

"Same night he croaked. Could have been after ten. I was just watching the news."

"What did he want?"

"Not me, that's for sure. The stupid bastard wanted to speak to Lida."

The lieutenant looked up. He suddenly remembered that he had forgotten to ask the giant's wife why she wasn't with her lover that night. After all, it had been a Wednesday. He said, "Did you call her to the phone?"

"Are you kidding?" growled the giant. "Of course not. I told him that if he tried phoning once more, I'd bust his jaw. Besides, Lida wasn't home anyway. She goes to see her mother every Wednesday."

"You believe that, do you?" said Malek.

The giant turned to him, a look of surprised suspicion growing in his eyes. "Her mother says so."

"She does, does she?" Malek pressed. "We've ascertained that your wife met Krasa every Wednesday evening. And your mother-in-law covered for them." Then he suddenly shouted, "And don't try to tell us you didn't know anything about it. Where were you Wednesday evening?"

But Malek's shout was drowned out by the wrestler's own outburst. "That fucking witch? And I fucking believed her! I'll— I'll—"

"Just relax, comrade," said Malek, taken aback. "Relax—"

.   .   .

"He doesn't look much like a killer to me," admitted Malek when they were back in the squad car. "More like a chump. On the other hand, he was out to get him. And he had two good reasons. Plus he's got no alibi."

"What do you mean, no alibi?" Pudil retorted. "He was watching the news on TV."

"By himself," said Malek. "He'd have to have a witness."

"He remembered what the news was. Not in much detail, but he knew they showed a delegation and a blast furnace. And a speech by some comrade, either in a collective farm or in the mines. It's just that he couldn't recall whether the comrade was Comrade Bilak or Indra or someone else. And besides that, he remembered the weather. Not what they said, but that there was a weather report." Pudil's voice trailed off.

The lieutenant reflected that listening to TV news alone was perhaps the easiest available alibi in Czechoslovakia. Unless a Kennedy was assassinated that day—

Malek came to the sergeant's aid. "If we can prove that Krasa really did call him—"

"That's it, comrade! The telephone call. We can check that at the exchange—"

"There's no way of tracing a local call," said the lieutenant, and couldn't resist another sarcastic comment. "That is, not unless the comrades from the Interior were tapping Sucharipa's line."

"Hardly." Pudil shook his head. "Sucharipa's a reliable comrade. There'd be no reason to plant a bug."

"But we can try asking at the Mermaid," said the old detective.

. . .

"I couldn't say for sure, gentlemen." The pub-keeper shook his head. "He may have made a call. He was one of the regulars—when they call, they just toss the money into a box by the phone. They never ask me first. As far as I know, no one's ever cheated."

The pub-keeper looked around nervously. It was early afternoon on a weekday and the pub was humming with activity. A waitress with two fists full of half-liter glass mugs was hurrying among the tables, and a waiter in a spattered white shirt was distributing bowls of tripe soup and plates of sausages and onions. The Vltava River was sparkling in the sun outside the window. The lieutenant couldn't concentrate for the life of him.

"Far as I know, only Nebesky called," said the pub-keeper. "I remember him standing by the telephone. But you know, things aren't as slow at night as they are this time of the day."

"What time did you see him call?"

"Oh, it must have been just before Krasa paid up and got ready to leave."

"Did you hear what Nebesky said? Or do you know who he called?"

"Are you kidding? In this racket?"

"What about the fellows Krasa was drinking with? What were they doing? Playing cards?"

"No, just drinking. And they were arguing about something."

"About what?"

"No idea. Evenings, I don't know where my own head is. We've got our hands full here, not like now. There's no time to sit and talk with the customers."

The harried waitress rushed by with twenty brimming beer mugs. Malek said, "But they were arguing?"

"I'm sure of that. Krasa finally lost his temper—at least, that's the impression I got. Then he left. He usually stayed longer."

. . .

"Well, well," remarked Malek when they were back in the car. "So our angel got into an argument."

"Speak no ill of the dead," said the sergeant. "That's why the comrades kept up that false front of solidarity. Of course, I criticized them for it. In Schoenfeld's case their solidarity was definitely out of place."

. . .

The question did not embarrass the wrestler's wife. "We'd arranged not to meet that evening. I'd promised my mother I'd go with her to visit my aunt. She's sick and alone at home."

"Naturally your mother and aunt will confirm that?" asked the sergeant.

"Why, certainly." The young woman looked surprised, and the sergeant squinted significantly at Boruvka and then at Malek. He met with two sphinxlike expressions and scowled.

"Did Schoenfeld—I mean Krasa—ever complain about conditions at work?"

Lida hesitated. "Well—the fact of the matter is, he wasn't too happy working at Humbug."

"Where?"

"I mean at Candy and Sweets. He called it Humbug. Ondra had a . . . sense of humor—" The young woman had to stop to fend off tears once more.

"What didn't he like about it?" asked Lieutenant Boruvka.

Lida was struggling with her emotions and didn't answer right away. The sergeant spoke instead: "The work was too tough for him, eh? It's no bed of roses, loading and unloading all day, dragging those boxes around to the stores. The comrade drivers told me what hard work it is."

"No, he never complained about that part of it," said Lida quickly. "He was used to hard work."

"He also got a bonus recently. Two hundred crowns, for being an exemplary worker," Malek put in bravely.

"That wasn't the first time," said the young woman. "But it was something else. He said the group he was working with wasn't—well, they weren't a good group, if you know what I mean."

An almost sardonic smile appeared on the face of the chairman of the SS Youth. Malek said quickly, "But his buddies told us he always stuck by the group."

"Well, that's—" The young woman swallowed. "He had, you know, very high standards—I mean, of honor and things like that. It came from spending so many years in—" and she looked uneasily at the grinning sergeant "—in that correctional institution. He said they all stuck together there."

"And here the comrades don't stick together, is that what you're trying to say?"

"I don't know. I only—I had the impression Ondra wasn't very fond of—the other drivers."

"Maybe they weren't too fond of him either, eh?" said the sergeant.

"I don't know. He never told me much. He just used to say that if it weren't for the fact that you were in prison, doing time was better than working for Humbug."

· · ·

"Why the hell *should* they be fond of him?" said Pudil angrily in the squad car. "They're all *real* workers, not the proletarized bourgeoisie that came out of the class struggle of the fifties, like him. And a Zionist to boot! Of course he fit in badly with the group."

"They claim differently."

"They're too polite. They lack Lenin's toughness. There are still leftovers from the past, even among workers. 'Speak no ill of the dead.' But when the dead man is someone like Shoenfeld, 'nothing ill' means either a lie or a pipe dream. Naturally he was an exemplary worker. How else could he penetrate their collective? That's the only way the enemy can worm their way in!"

"And after all," said the lieutenant, "the whole collective is exemplary. We found out they all get bonuses. Why should Krasa be unpopular with them for being an exemplary worker as well?"

The sergeant shot an offended glance at the lieutenant. "You don't understand, comrade?"

The lieutenant only shrugged his shoulders.

"It was most likely something else about him that spoiled their relationship. Probably something to do with his world view, if you ask me."

The old detective thought for a minute, then said quietly, "You may be right, comrade."

. . .

"An argument? With Ondra?" Jindra Nebesky was flabbergasted.

"That's what the pub-keeper says."

"Why should we argue? We were the best of friends. Anyway, Ondra was as mild as a lamb."

"The pub-keeper says Krasa left the pub early because of an argument with you two."

"What can I say?" Nebesky shook his head.

Suddenly Kudelka whispered, "Jindra—" He seemed nervous to the lieutenant. In the few minutes they had been standing there in the garage with a small group of drivers, Kudelka had smoked two cigarettes and was working on his third. "Unless it was about—"

"About what?" asked the detective.

"About—you know—Lida." The lieutenant's experienced ears recognized clearly the voice of a prompter. But for a long time Nebesky said nothing and the old detective made no attempt to break the silence. Finally the driver said, "Oh, *that!*"

"What?" barked Malek.

"It was nothing," said Kudelka. "We just made fun of him. But in a friendly way. We weren't nasty about it."

"But he got mad anyway?"

"Well—sort of mad. We were ribbing him because—like, we didn't know he'd be coming to the pub that night—that is, we weren't expecting him."

"Why not?" asked the lieutenant.

"Because he used to see her every Wednesday night. Lida, I mean."

"Then what was he doing in the pub that particular Wednesday?"

The question seemed to bring Nebesky to life again. "We asked him the same thing. He said Lida was off visiting a sick aunt. So I says, 'How do you know it's not a sick uncle and how do you know the uncle's not in the pink and are you sure it's just an uncle?' Dumb stuff like that. And he got sore."

"Was that all there was to it?"

"Well, I guess we did lay it on a little thick. You know, told him to ditch her, that kind of thing. We said she didn't wait for him last time and she'd dump him again when they got married, stuff like that. Stupid ribbing, I admit it. Poor bugger, we made his last night miserable."

"It's not your fault, comrades," said the sergeant. "He had it coming to him, seducing another comrade's wife."

"By the way," the lieutenant interrupted, turning to Nebesky, "who did you call just before Krasa left the pub?"

The driver obviously didn't expect the question. He coughed, then cleared his throat.

"I called Olda," he said and cleared his throat again. "I—wanted him to—to bring his—set of wrenches to work the next day."

"Olda?"

"That's me." A fellow with a pale face got up from the workbench. "Olda Huml. But I wasn't home."

Malek looked around sharply and then turned to Nebesky. "So you haven't got a witness to that telephone call?" Then, *"As you were!"* he shouted at himself, "Yes he does, he's got the pub-keeper." He spun to face Huml instead. "But you," he roared, *"you* don't have an alibi!"

"My father was home," said Huml. "He told Nebesky I was at Karel Bousek's place. So Jindra called me there."

"And what were you doing at Bousek's?" asked Malek, sheepish at his outburst.

"We were playing cards with Zbynek—I mean Cespiva," Huml replied, looking around the garage. "Karel's not here yet, but you can ask him. He lives in that highrise on Lookout Hill."

"Is that a co-op building?" asked the lieutenant.

For a moment there was silence. Then Nebesky said, "No, those are the new flats they've put straight onto the private market. Karel has a three-bedroom—" Nebesky's voice trailed off and there was silence once more.

"Who does Krasa's route now?" asked the lieutenant.

"Me," said Kudelka.

. . .

At the office of Candy and Sweets the lieutenant asked for a list of the stores the dead driver had delivered to. He was given several lists—obviously Krasa had frequently been transferred from route to route. Perhaps because he was such an exemplary worker. Perhaps because he wanted to penetrate the collective.

The old detective wondered.

. . .

"Hell, I really put my foot in it over those telephone calls," lamented Malek in the squad car. "I knew the pub-keeper had seen him and I go asking him for witnesses—and Huml's not even under suspicion. He's got no motive and I—"

"You didn't put your foot in it at all, Pavel," said the lieutenant. "You were right to ask. There are too many of those phone calls and they've got too many witnesses and they're all too dependable."

"What do you mean by that, comrade first lieutenant?" asked Pudil, annoyed. "Are you suggesting workers would lie?"

"People do lie," said the lieutenant gloomily. "After all, you don't consider Lida Sucharipa's mother and sick aunt as dependable witnesses."

"But that's something else altogether. We know the mother was part of the conspiracy—"

"What did you say, comrade?" asked the old detective with interest. "Conspiracy?"

"Well, okay, maybe it's not the right word. What I mean is, she aided and abetted their screwing around."

"But maybe it is the right word," said the lieutenant.

Malek looked at him in surprise.

"Though probably not for the activities that make for a divorce action," added the lieutenant.

. . .

That night, as usual in the past few years, the old detective had trouble getting to sleep. Through the open bedroom window the smell of flowers drifted in from Mala Strana, and also the faint strains of *Eine kleine Nachtmusik,* played by a string orchestra in the Ledeburske Gardens. But over the melody of the violins he could hear something else—an oft-played record coming from Zuzana's room. The sound was muffled but clear enough to the lieutenant's attentive ear:

> Help me, Information,
> Get in touch with my Marie;
> She's the only one who'd phone me here
> From Memphis, Tennessee. . . .

The lieutenant couldn't sleep. In his mind he saw the lanky young man in his blue jeans, now his son-in-law, in a city he had never seen and would never in his life see, a city that bore the name of a famous brand of prewar cigarettes. Once, in a fit of holy indignation, the venerable Father Meloun had confiscated a packet of them from him. And then the usual ghostly procession of cases passed through the old detective's troubled mind—all solved yet unresolved, thanks to the vagaries of justice. Or rather, class justice. The procession was led by a chalk-white dancer, followed by a skull with several teeth missing, then by female legs and arms in an almost aesthetic ornament. . . . The lieutenant was suddenly afraid he would go mad and do something that . . .

> Marie, she's so very young,
> So Information, please,

Try to put me through to her
In Memphis, Tennessee. . . .

Lieutenant Boruvka's heart almost stopped beating under its terrible burden of sadness.

.   .   .

"I'd like a hundred grams of Italian Mix," he said next morning to the white-haired lady behind the counter in a fussy little sweet-shop in Mala Strana. It was 8:30 and he was the first customer.

"A hundred grams of Italian Mix coming up, sir," sang the old lady in an unsteady voice, ladling up the candies from a bin with a chrome-plated scoop. She sifted them out into a paper bag on the scales and then, with her little finger—on which the lieutenant noticed a blackened fingernail—she pushed small pieces of chocolate from the scoop into the bag until the needle came to rest at a hundred grams.

She made sure it was the full hundred, perhaps because the customer was watching her so intently.

"That will be three-ninety, please." She smiled at the old detective.

The lieutenant didn't return her smile. He reached into his pocket and, instead of money, pulled out a hundred-gram weight. He lifted the bag off the scales and replaced it with the weight.

"Sir, what are you—" The old lady made a feeble protest but her guilty conscience was too obvious. The detective gently pushed aside the wrinkled hand reaching for the weight. The needle of the scales came to rest at 120 grams and the old lady turned white.

The lieutenant looked at her reproachfully. He pulled his badge out of his pocket and held it so that she could see it. Instead her eyes closed, and he just managed to catch her before she hit the floor. Then he carried her into the storage space behind the shop and put her in a chair until she regained consciousness.

.   .   .

"Whenever they come," she said, "they always say, 'I'm in a terrible hurry today, ma'am. I've got ten more stores to do before closing!' And then they start heaving the boxes into the store-room and I haven't got time to count them and then they give me the invoice to sign and say, 'Come on, lady, don't give us a hard time, count them later. If there's anything missing, just let me know next week.' And there's *always* something missing."

The old lady began to cry.

"And do you tell them?"

"Yes, of course. And they just laugh at me. They say I'm an old woman and my eyes are bad. One time they counted the boxes as they unloaded them and the count was right. But then I weighed the boxes and they were all short."

"Why don't you report this to the head office?"

"I do, but they always brush me off and tell me I'll have to prove the delivery men are responsible. Once I told them to send someone to check and, wouldn't you know it, the very next day they sent a comrade from head office who hid out in front when they came, and that day everything was right."

The lieutenant nodded sadly. "So you started to steal from the customers."

"Oh, my God, sir, I had to. I've got to hand over all our cash received and it has to be correct, right down to the last heller. Anything short comes off my wages—and with what I'm getting, it would take half my pay just to make up the difference."

She was overwhelmed by a new fit of sobbing.

"What about Mr. Krasa—did you complain to him too?"

The old lady wiped her eyes and looked into the lieutenant's moon-shaped face. "I told him about it, yes. Because after he started making deliveries, it all stopped. He seemed like a decent young man, so I told him what had been going on and he promised to look into it. And about a week after that they transferred him to another route and it started all over again. Maybe he was just talking, or maybe there was nothing he could do. It's not easy standing up to those crooks—"

"So you doctored the scales and started cheating again?"

"Please, sir, don't report me. I'll try and make it up to the customers, even if I have to die of starvation. I know almost all my customers in person."

"There's no need to be upset," said the lieutenant. "I guarantee you that matters will soon be put right." He hesitated, then added, "There's more at stake than a few grams of Italian Mix."

. . .

From the division, he called the State Office of Inspection and gave them several clear instructions. Next he ordered Malek and Pudil to go to the Price Inspection Bureau and personally ensure that his orders were properly carried out. Then he went to the police garage, signed out an unmarked Skoda MB, and drove into the city.

On the seat beside him was the map of another route, which he had obtained in the Candy and Sweets office the day before. He looked at his watch, then drove to the candy shop in Konev Street and parked a short distance away. About a quarter of an hour later the delivery truck pulled up to the shop. On the sides of the truck were crude paintings of ice-cream bars, chocolates, and cakes. A wiry driver jumped out, opened the doors at the back of the truck, picked up an armful of boxes, and disappeared into the store. When he walked back through the shop to the truck, the lieutenant was standing at the counter ordering a hundred grams of humbugs. He looked grimly at the driver and the man recognized him immediately.

"Oh, morning, lieutenant," he said, turning slightly pale. Then he added conventionally—although it didn't sound like a convention—"How are things going?"

"All right," said the lieutenant gloomily.

"Well, I—excuse me, lieutenant, but I'm in a terrible rush. I've got eight more stores to do today," said an embarrassed Svata Kudelka, and rushed for the exit.

"Don't let me keep you," said the lieutenant, glowering like a thundercloud.

Then he paid for the humbugs, got into the Skoda MB, consulted the map on the seat beside him, and drove, at the greatest possible legal speed, to Zukov Street.

. . .

When Svata Kudelka saw the lieutenant in the Zukov Street shop, somberly watching the attendant weigh out a hundred grams of humbugs, he turned white.

"What a coincidence—isn't it?" he said.

"It is," agreed the detective. "Better get a move on so you can make it to those other stores—how many are left, seven?"

Kudelka tried to respond but finally said nothing. He left the store like a walking ghost.

. . .

In the shop on Tolbuchin Street the driver reeled, leaned against the counter, and stared at the lieutenant without even making an effort to say anything. So it was Boruvka who spoke first.

"Shall we go?" he asked. He paid for his hundred grams of humbugs and led the driver, now dripping with sweat, to the Skoda MB. They left the delivery van parked in the street. The lieutenant noticed that under the crudely drawn ice-cream bar someone had chalked in a faded word: HUMBUG.

It was like an epitaph.

. . .

"He simply gave them an ultimatum," Boruvka said that evening to Malek and Pudil. "He had served his term with criminals and murderers. As you know, in our correctional institutions we don't separate Krasa's kind from the hardened criminals." The sergeant was evidently getting ready to respond, so the detective hurried to finish what he wanted to say. "Perhaps it's democratic, but it gave Krasa a hatred—or rather, a need to have nothing more to do with such people. And then he got his job with Humbug and realized his co-workers were exactly the sort of people he'd learned to loathe in jail. According to Kudelka, when old Mrs. Souckova complained to him he went to the other drivers with an ultimatum. He said, 'If you were stealing from the state, maybe I'd keep quiet. But you're stealing from old women—' "

"There, you see, comrade lieutenant? Stealing from the state, which means from all of us—that wouldn't have bothered him."

"Yes," admitted the lieutenant, "ideologically that was hardly the correct attitude. But after all, he was a proletarized bourgeois, as you know. Anyway, he gave them an ultimatum. They tried to bribe him but he refused."

"Because he was afraid!" burst out Pudil. "Not because he was such a holier-than-thou angel! He knew that our correctional institutions are no holiday camps!"

"Subjective motivation—as you'll certainly agree, comrade—does not count," said the lieutenant. "What counts is what a man does."

Pudil snorted, but his Marxism failed him.

"The other drivers even invited him to join their—" he hesitated, then said it "—their gang. A number of shop managers were members; these managers received the goods stolen from the other stores. Then they split the profits." He paused and then, against his will, added, "In America they call it racketeering."

He paused, waiting for Pudil's reaction, but the SS chairman only scowled.

"Anyway, he gave them this ultimatum," continued Lieutenant Boruvka, "and they decided to get rid of him. Bousek did the job. By the way, that was what put me on the right track: a delivery boy who can afford to buy a flat on the free market? And a three-bedroom one, yet? An apartment like that costs as least a hundred thousand. Probably more."

"Why shouldn't a driver be able to buy a flat?" growled Pudil. "We're certainly not putting them up for the bourgeoisie."

"Could you afford it, man?" Malek blurted with unusual bitterness. He, like so many others, hadn't had the lieutenant's luck; he was on the wrong end of a long waiting list for a flat in the housing co-operative. "Or me?" he said. "And I'm not a bourgeois either. My father was a shoemaker who got ruined in the Depression by competition from the Bata company."

The SS chairman was silent. He was a graduate of several courses, but they had all been crash courses, and the case, from a class point of view, was obviously too complicated for him. The lieutenant went on.

"They knew that every Wednesday Krasa walked Lida home

before eleven o'clock. Bousek was going to wait for him near where
the Sucharipas lived. They were supposed to be playing cards—
to give Bousek an alibi—at Huml's place, but Huml's father unexpectedly showed up on a visit. So they got up and went to Bousek's place, but they didn't have time to get word to the other two
who were establishing their alibis in the Mermaid. Then a second
thing happened that they weren't prepared for: Krasa showed up
at the Mermaid at eight o'clock. That's why Nebesky called—first
to Huml's place and then, when Huml's father told him where
they were, to Bousek's. They made a quick change of plan and
one of them drove to the street where Sucharipa lives to pick up
the waiting Bousek. He took him to Nusle Gardens because that's
the way Krasa had to walk back from the pub."

The lieutenant lit a cigar. There was still no reaction from Pudil.

"So it wasn't Lida they were arguing about," said the detective.
"It was Krasa's ultimatum. And it wasn't Krasa who called
Sucharipa, it was Nebesky. All he had to do was disguise his voice
a little. Sucharipa was not what you'd call bright. But they had to
make sure Lida wasn't already home, because they had an idea.
They knew that Sucharipa was jealous of Krasa and that Krasa
had beaten him up. It worked right into their plan: Sucharipa
would have no alibi, being at home alone, but he had a motive
and he's a metal-worker. And they planned to kill Krasa with a
hammer."

The hour of five struck from a nearby church tower. The lieutenant looked out the window. In a nest above a little-known
saint, two young pigeons were getting ready to make their first
flight.

"Very well," said Pudil in an annoyed tone. "They're a bunch
of chumps and an embarrassment to the working class. And they
have to be justly but harshly punished."

The lieutenant looked at the small, scowling face of the confused idealist.

"If it makes you feel any better, comrade," he said, "stealing
from old lady shopkeepers was just a sideline. The real operation

was a big one. The company director himself was involved. And even—" he glanced at Pudil out of the corner of his eye and almost felt sorry for him, so he decided to buck him up "—even Comrade Roth, the Party secretary. For example, a whole wagonload of cocoa got lost—"

The sergeant suddenly went red in the face and was gripped by a fierce outburst of hatred, undoubtedly of the class variety. "What a bloody mess!" he shouted. "They made a real pigsty out of the country in just nine months, those filthy Dubcekists. Revisionists, all of them! It's going to take *years* to set things right again!"

. . .

This time the little fish from the Paraná River were satisfied; the lieutenant's conscience remained calm and no one else joined the pale procession in his night dreams. Yet still he had trouble sleeping. Into the August night of his inner hearing (or was it from his daughter's room?) he heard a young man in blue jeans calling across the distances from a city whose name smelled of those cigarettes confiscated ages ago by the venerable Father Meloun. . . .

> Help me, Information,
> Can't ask for more, but please!
> You don't know how I miss her
> In Memphis, Tennessee. . . .

The old detective had a miserable feeling that the young man was calling out in vain.

Pirates

The fatal wound was unusual. "A blow from the left side," said Dr. Seifert, "probably by a blunt object; but I can't quite figure it out. It doesn't look like the object was hard. A rubber truncheon, maybe, but the mark seems too narrow for that. It's strange."

The corpse was strange as well. It lay, still warm, in the dark stairwell of an eighteenth-century tenement house in Mala Strana. Sergeant Pudil was leaning keenly over it, examining the head, which was cocked at an unnatural angle against the right shoulder. Lieutenant Boruvka suddenly realized that he felt nothing at all towards the murdered old man, and he was ashamed at his own callousness. There had been a time, not so long ago, when each murder victim seemed like a tragically unfinished novel. But the old man with the broken neck awakened other sensations in him; it was as though someone, in a fit of rage, had tried to destroy evidence of his political past.

The sergeant looked up from the corpse. "I'll be hanged if it isn't karate, comrade. They showed us exactly the same kind of bruises in the course."

. . .

This sentence was still ringing in the lieutenant's ears as the super-intendent opened the door to the dead man's flat. The sergeant looked around like an animal sniffing the wind. The apartment consisted of a kitchen and one room which was dominated by a large certificate in a frame, the kind that used to enclose portraits of aristocratic ladies.

> THE PRAGUE COMMITTEE
> OF THE UNION OF CZECHOSLOVAK-SOVIET
> FRIENDSHIP
> TAKES GREAT PLEASURE IN NAMING
> FRANTISEK NOVOTNY
> AN HONORARY MEMBER ON THE OCCASION
> OF HIS SEVENTY-FIFTH BIRTHDAY

There were no other certificates on the walls. The document seemed rather slender recognition for a lifetime of dedication, the lieutenant reflected. What had the dead man been?

"He worked in an office at the Ministry of Heavy Industry," the superintendent told them. "But he's been retired for fifteen years. He worked for another eight or so, then it got too much for him and he packed it in."

The sergeant lifted a strange object from the table and held it up in the light streaming into the room through a dirty window. The object glistened. It was a bronzed bust made of papier-mâché, a kind he had not seen—at least not in public—for a long time. The sergeant stared respectfully at the lackluster bust of Stalin. Then, along with the lieutenant, he looked at the wall opposite the framed certificate. On it hung a portrait of the late Klement Gottwald, the man officially known as the first working-class pres-ident, who had died of "Moscow flu" just days after the demise of his mentor, Josef Stalin.

Above a writing table there was yet another devotional portrait from the official pantheon: a photograph, to which a black band of mourning had been affixed across the lower left-hand corner. The lieutenant didn't know who the man in the photograph was, and was just about to ask the superintendent when he heard Malek behind him saying, "Josef! Take a gander at this!"

The lieutenant turned around. Malek was holding something even more unusual than the bust of Stalin, something vaguely resembling an army radio receiver with two sets of wires running out of it, one ending in earphones, the other in a flat, circular object with a rubber ring around it. It was this that Malek was holding out for the lieutenant.

But the sergeant got there first. Eagerly he grasped the earphones and shot a glance at Malek, who quickly handed him the whole device. The sergeant, though obviously unfamiliar with this technology, was as usual undeterred by his own ignorance. Frowning, he put the flat round rubber object to his eye and peered inside. The old detective let him examine the rubbery darkness for a while before remarking, "It's a listening device. There's a special microphone inside the plate that can pick up a conversation through a three-foot wall. That rubber rim is a suction device for attaching . . ."

"Well, I'll be!" whistled the sergeant. "So he was a . . . and the karate . . . Comrades! It all fits together! The karate! Do you see?"

The only response from the others was silence. The lieutenant donned his sphinxlike expression—something he did rather frequently these days, though it looked more like an uncomprehending moon. Malek wore the look of a retarded country bumpkin and Dr. Seifert's face was the mask of a man whose expertise is in a different field altogether.

"Look, you've got the karate, you've got this counterespionage device, you've got the former employee of a vital ministry, you put it all together and . . ."

He looked around and saw a shadow of suspicion cross the lieutenant's neutral mask.

"All right. I know. I was a little too hasty about that Zionist.

And I admitted it, too, in the spirit of self-criticism. But then there was no listening device, no karate, just a hammer. . . ."

The sergeant hesitated. He had made many overly hasty judgments in almost two years of service with Lieutenant Boruvka and each time he had owned up. Once he had even inflicted a minor gunshot wound on a man he was arresting—inappropriately rather than mistakenly, as it later turned out—for murder. When the man had reached into his breast pocket in the familiar gesture of one about to display his badge, the sergeant, who had a secret passion for the American westerns that had recently flooded the cinemas to replace Vera Chytilova's formalistic films, interpreted the man's movement à la OK Corral. He got his shot away—or so he thought—as quickly as the Sundance Kid, but fortunately not as accurately, so that ultimately the sister security organization was not deprived of a rather important hitman. Sergeant Pudil was reprimanded but allowed to remain in the lieutenant's group, despite the old detective's suggestion that he be transferred to Petty Theft. The incident had badly shaken the sergeant's self-confidence, but instead of knuckling under, he intensified his efforts, driven by the hope of one day capturing James Bond—whom the sergeant, having been misled by references to Bond in the leading Party newspaper, believed to be a real person, a colleague from the far shore.

Now the lieutenant had taken him somewhat aback, and he was worried about having to submit to another round of self-criticism. But he restored his confidence by examining the certificate in the gold frame, then the deceased president, and finally the generalissimo's bust. As his conviction grew, he took the special microphone by the cord and, swinging it round like a slingshot, looked at the photograph with the mourning band. Lieutenant Boruvka, Malek, Dr. Seifert, and the superintendent followed the journey of his eyes until the superintendent could hold back no longer.

"That's Comrade Jidas," he said. "They were friends. Comrade Jidas was one of that group that invited in the Soviets. . . ."

"That clinches it," said Sergeant Pudil, this time with utter conviction.

.   .   .

In the next flat on the left lived a couple called the Blazeks, but
they only interested the sergeant for a moment. As soon as the
superintendent told him who lived in the flat on the right, all his
most intrinsic abilities were aroused. He put the earphones on
and began listening through the wall.

"There's a bunch of people in there and they're all talking at
once," he reported. "And it's anti-state talk."

"Is that a fact?" said the lieutenant with insincere surprise. "In
that case, I'd better look into it alone. They won't feel they have
to pretend in front of me. I . . . ," he explained hastily, "I happen
to know Kopanec. His niece used to work with me before she got
married. Kopanec trusts me completely. I'll just sort of drop in—
by chance. We mustn't arouse their suspicions. . . ."

"The bastards!" exploded the sergeant. "They're insulting our
first working-class pres . . ."

"Off I go," said the lieutenant quickly. "I'll take care of it myself.
You go back to headquarters and . . . and . . ." He could hardly
get it past his lips, for a sudden terror came over him—a terror
that came from a longing to help where he had no business doing
so, at least, not as a member of the Public Security force. But
there was that old record in his daughter's room, played so often
during the past two years that he could scarcely understand the
words any more. "And phone the comrades at Interior. Ask them
to send you material on Novotny . . . and on the Blazeks too, of
course. And everyone in the building. The comrade here will give
you a list. . . ."

He nodded towards the superintendent, but the sergeant said,
"We're going in there with you, comrade!"

It sounded almost like a threat. A wave of red anger swept
through the old detective and he roared back at his subordinate,
"You're going to phone Interior. And that's an order. And I'm a
first lieutenant, in case you've forgotten, comrade sergeant!"

The two years Pudil had spent in the company of his mild-mannered superior officer had not prepared him for such an outburst. But the Pavlovian reflex worked and he blurted, "Yes sir, comrade first lieutenant!"

．．．

"Well, I do declare!" said the writer through the half-open door. Somewhere above him, the doorbell was tinkling a phrase from "Ach, du lieber Augustin." As usual, the writer was mildly tipsy. "You haven't come to put the cuffs on me again, have you, lieutenant? Last time you didn't get very far, but now I'd like to confess up front, without the torture, if you don't mind. I have a very low threshold of pain."

"Can I talk to you alone, Master?" whispered the lieutenant.

Kopanec chuckled. "Won't be 'master' for quite a while yet. I'm still a mere tyro. Digging the new subway. There are no master craftsmen in that field . . . just laborers."

"It's about a serious matter. Can we discuss it alone for a bit?"

Kopanec looked around. A company of intoxicated men and women was sitting in the room on the floor, the coffee table, and the sideboard were strewn with bottles, some opened, some still corked. Except for a dim light cast by some candles and, in the corner, a dark red Chinese lantern bearing the portrait of Mao Tse Tung, the room was almost dark.

"*The Lonely Crowd,*" intoned Kopanec. "And here we are in that crowd, alone. That's the safest way in these times, lieutenant."

"Shh!" said the lieutenant in alarm. "Call me . . . call me Novak, let's say," he whispered. "It's a delicate business. I don't want . . ."

Kopanec turned towards the room and announced ceremoniously, "Comrades, I'd like you to meet a rare and precious guest. Mr. Novak. A former physical education teacher. At present without permanent employment. An old and trusted friend of mine, so you can carry on talking to your heart's content."

Several people raised their wine glasses and a man whose face was vaguely familiar to the lieutenant resumed talking, probably where he had left off when he had been interrupted by the lieutenant's knock.

"I treat it like a traffic accident. It's a shock at first, but sooner or later you have to get over it. I say you only have the moral right to leave the country if your life's in actual danger."

"By the time you find that out, it's always too late, isn't it?" said a woman. She didn't look old, but her hair was prematurely gray.

"Those days are over, Sarka," said the speaker earnestly. "Today even *they* know you can't undo a knot with a sword. . . ."

"When you've got a chronic kidney problem like me," said a bald-headed man, "two years in the cooler can knock twenty years off your life."

"You should worry," said the woman called Sarka. "Keep on hitting the booze like that and your chronic kidneys won't last two years. In the sunshine."

The lieutenant listened, fascinated. Kopanec took him by the arm. "Leave them be. As usual, they're trying to square the circle. In my opinion, it's a bloody mess no matter what you call it—car accident or cultural genocide. I'm an expert on bloody messes. And I say we're all buried in shit right up to here—Prague, San Francisco, it doesn't matter a damn."

He led the lieutenant to a dark corner where two armchairs sat buried under stacks of yellowed magazines. The writer carefully lifted the magazines and put them down on the carpet. The lieutenant saw that they were old copies of something called *The Occult Review*.

"I've taken up science," Kopanec explained. "Nowadays the daily press specializes in pure mysticism, so I thought, what the hell, and borrowed these from my great-grandmother. You didn't happen to know my great-grandfather, by any chance? Ran a clairvoyance lab in Nerudova Street. Those were the days, by God," he sighed, pouring the lieutenant and himself a drink from a bottle that was only available in the foreign-currency shops. "Greatgrandad was in the slammer during the war. The Nazis shut down scientific operations like his, as you know, but he kept at it on the sly. He was a cautious old bugger, but his destiny caught up with him in the end. Ah, well." He sighed, and they touched glasses.

"Did he survive the war?" asked the lieutenant considerately.

The expert in bloody messes appeared not to have heard the question.

"Once they stuck an informer in with him. Granddad knew the guy was a stool pigeon, so he told his fortune, predicted he'd get to be an *Oberscharführer* in the Saint Wenceslas SS Division. A bad psychological mistake that was, because by that time the war was in its dying days and a career in the SS was the furthest thing from the fink's mind. What he wanted to know was whether he was going to keep his neck out of a noose after the war, and he was pissed off because he thought Granddad was having some fun at his expense. But anyway, he survived."

"Who, your great-granddad?" asked the lieutenant, while trying to think of the most considerate—and tactful—way to inform the writer that the noose, or at least arrest, was now threatening *him*.

"You kidding? He wouldn't lay off, read the screws' palms in prison and they hanged him for it. It was the informer who survived. Never got to be an *Oberscharführer*, but I hear he's not so badly off. I have an idea," and he squinted with malicious delight at the lieutenant, "that he's even a colleague of yours. At least, that's my impression. He's titular head of some department in the Historical Institute, but, I mean . . ."

The lieutenant gave his standard, automatic response: "I'm with the *criminal* police. That's why I'm here."

"Oh, dearie me! Don't tell me another girl's in trouble? But the girls don't swarm around me the way they used to, lieutenant. Not since I've been swinging a pick for a living. I don't mean to suggest they discriminate on the basis of class, not at all. But you know how it is, I just haven't got the personal charm of a man like Vrchcolab." And the master of bloody messes glanced enviously at the man holding court in the living room. "They won't do you the pleasure," the bald man was just saying to him. "You've got too high a profile. There's no percentage in making world-famous martyrs any more. Even they know that by now."

The lieutenant shuddered. He remembered where he knew Vrchcolab from: he was always being attacked in the papers.

Boruvka admired the man's courage. Once again, he felt those man-eating fish from the Paraná River nipping away at his conscience.

"That's precisely why I do what I do. The world must be told what's going on here."

"What world do you mean?" asked the bald man. "The one that lounges about by the swimming pool with a newspaper in one hand and a mint julep in the other? What other world is there?"

The lieutenant listened again, fascinated. "So tell me about it," he heard Kopanec's voice say. "Another ballerina? Otherwise I'm not interested."

With great effort, the old detective turned his attention from his private thoughts back to objective reality and said, "It's your neighbor. He's been murdered. And . . . ," he lowered his whisper until it was scarcely audible, "I have reason to suspect—in fact I'm practically certain—that he worked for . . . the organization I *don't* belong to. There was a bugging device in his flat. He was probably listening to what you were saying here when . . ."

"No matter," said the writer calmly. "There's already a microphone over there in the radiator and another one in the telephone."

The lieutenant was visibly shaken and the writer slapped himself on the forehead. "Oh Christ!" He lowered his voice to a whisper even less audible than the lieutenant's. "A thousand pardons. I guess they haven't got you on tape yet, have they? God the last thing I want to do is get you in trouble. . . ."

He got up, took the phone off the hook, and tossed a thick blanket over the radiator. The lieutenant's knees began to tremble. "Normally we don't bother any more, because they can hardly find out anything about us they don't already know." He looked around at the company and so did the lieutenant. Once again, his attention was drawn to Vrchcolab.

"It doesn't matter if not a soul *over there* takes any notice," he was saying. "The important thing is that it be said *here!*"

"To guarantee yourself a place in history, right?" said the bald man sarcastically.

"So it won't vanish from history altogether," Vrchcolab shot back.

The lieutenant was ashamed that he couldn't control the trembling of his own limbs. He wasn't a coward. He had proven this again and again in situations that were a matter of life and death, not just of prison. But now he was afraid. On those occasions he had always stood alone with a pistol, facing someone who was also alone with a pistol. The odds were even. Now he was afraid. Kopanec whispered into his ear, "I'd feel awful if you were to get in trouble over this. I know you're a good man. My niece Eva told me a lot about you. There was once a time, if I'm not mistaken, when she was nuts over you. But I don't suppose you're interested in such things. You're a lucky man. Eva's already had two kids with that brain surgeon of hers, did you know?"

The lieutenant was afraid. At the mention of the progeny of the former policewoman with the magnificent chignon, he realized that it was not for himself that he was afraid. *People can be brought to heel if they are afraid and have a lot of children.* . . . In his mind he heard the voice of the sweat-soaked writer, and he began to tremble. "Really? I'm glad to hear it," he said sincerely, though somewhat absently. "And I . . . I was fond of your niece, too, I won't deny it. But she . . ."

"Maybe you didn't say anything improper," the writer interrupted him, once again speaking in that microphonophobic whisper. "Or did you? What did you say, anyway?"

"Nothing. Unless . . . ," and the lieutenant adjusted his whisper to match Kopanec's, "as I told you, the murdered man worked for the Ministry of the Interior. . . ."

"You said that in a whisper. I know for a fact that the mike won't pick up whispers when others are speaking out loud in the same room, like now. What a racket!"

"You're no better than a collaborator!" someone was shouting.

"You act in those shit-bag plays of theirs while others can't even get a foot in the door any more!"

"Isn't he wonderful? You'd be delighted to act in those shit-bag plays if only they'd let you, darling!"

The lieutenant had to agree that a conversation of such intensity must have drowned out his incriminating remark.

"Who do you think did him in?" whispered Kopanec.

The old detective shrugged his shoulders and asked, "No one left here in the last hour or so?"

"No. This bunch has been here since six."

"Not even briefly?"

"I'm sure of it. The john's inside here, not on the balcony, and I've got those chimes on the main entrance. Kind of a joke. I bought them in Vienna once. Those were the days, I tell you. *Ach, du lieber Augustin!*" he recited dreamily, then suddenly spat out, "*Alles ist hin!*" He shook his head resolutely. "I'd have noticed if anyone left. That song is becoming a royal pain in the ass, I should disconnect the goddamn thing." He looked at the lieutenant. "What is it? Did you think of something?"

The lieutenant had fallen into a trancelike state that signaled profound thought. As if in a dream, he asked, "Are you absolutely sure your flat is bugged?"

"Want to bet it isn't? But I can't take bets on that, it wouldn't be fair. Of course it's bugged." He was still whispering. "Once— about a year after the fraternal assistance brigades rode their tanks into town—the cops called me in for some friendly little interrogations. Went on for about a month, and they'd play me tapes with scenes from my older domestic performances, even before the invasion. Some of them involved a certain young lady. They were okay, only mildly anti-state and only occasionally. But once they played me a monologue—I had no idea myself I'd ever uttered anything so enlightened. Of course, I was looped at the time, which, as we know is not an extenuating circumstance in our scientifically established state—and rightly so. I still don't know why they didn't throw the book at me."

"I don't understand it," said the lieutenant.

"Neither do I," said Kopanec. "When Tony Novotny was president—may the good Lord grant him eternal glory—I would have got a year, probably more."

"That's not what I mean. There's something else I don't understand."

"I don't understand any of it," said Kopanec, taking a drink. "I don't understand a goddamn thing any more, my dear lieutenant."

"God, how our holy émigrés carry on!" another voice was shouting. "They leave the country, they live like pigs in clover, and instead of turning their back and saying 'good riddance!' they can't stop writing about us. The bastards probably make their living at it, so they make damn good and sure the interest doesn't dry up on them."

"You sound like an editorial in *Tribuna,*" said Sarka.

"Occasionally something with a grain of truth to it gets into *Tribuna* by mistake," the drunken voice went on. "The sooner the emigrants shit on us and get off the pot, the sooner the Commies will lay off and let us get on with it."

"Get on with shit," said the bald man. "Not that I have anything against shit. But during the so-called years of deformation, your line was 'complete freedom or nothing,' because without absolute freedom, you can only do what's permitted. You even let them quote you in the Western press, and that was at a time when I was saying privately that it's better to have what's permitted than nothing at all. Well, now you've got your nothing; so what the fuck are you complaining about?"

"I don't hold it against anyone for leaving," said another voice. "I can understand that. Some people were afraid nothing could be done. . . ."

"They were afraid they'd end up in Siberia, the heroes," shouted another drunken voice. "Now they're all cozy and safe and they've got courage to burn. At home, while we were trying to get things moving, they collaborated!"

"You tried so hard to get things moving they gave you a state prize," said the bald man, "while they were hounding me for existentialism."

"No, no, there's something else," the lieutenant was whispering. "Perhaps you can help me."

"Me? I can't even help myself," said the famous writer sadly.

"Look, he was working for . . . for *them*. He must have known you had a permanent bug in your flat, so it's not logical that he would have listened to you with a portable device."

The writer gave him a dumb look. "Maybe he was just eager."

"Maybe," said the lieutenant. "But who are those people living on the other side?"

"Someone called Blazek and his wife. Pensioners."

"Pensioners?" The lieutenant thought for a moment. The murdered man had been a pensioner too, his head oddly bent towards his right shoulder. Karate? Perhaps. What sort of person would be likely to know karate in this country? "How old are they?"

"Don't know, exactly, but over seventy for sure."

"What kind of shape are they in, physically?"

"The old geezer has asthma. Takes him about an hour to walk up to the third floor. That's in summer. Takes him twice as long in winter. His wife seems a little more chipper, but she's got rheumatism in her lower back or something. She looks like she's been gathering mushrooms all her life. She walks bent over at right angles."

Karate! But why was he listening in on them? They don't hand out bugging devices just to find out if two old people tottering on the brink of the grave are fulsome enough in their praise of the first secretary.

"They do *not* live like pigs in clover over there," said a woman's voice, one the lieutenant had not yet heard. "They have to work hard for what they get. My husband, for example, works every other weekend. . . ."

"What did you marry him for then, if he's such a poor, exploited wretch? And anyway, he's a Kraut," said a stout young man.

"I'm not complaining," the girl shot back. "I just mentioned him to demonstrate that your eyes are bigger than your brains. Things aren't all that great in the West either, you know."

"Hey, hey, none of that, now!" said another voice. "You've turned into an agent of socialism over there, Jaruska. Go on back to Paris, where it's still fashionable to talk like that."

"Oh God, you're all being so impossible!" said the girl. "I'm good for sending you ten LPs a month, aren't I? You have any idea how much they cost? And new dresses from Printemps for your darling Bohuna so the poor dear won't suffer. And even so, she badmouths me. She tells all her friends I buy them at the fleamarket because she thinks only Schiaparellis are good enough for her."

"And don't you buy clothes at the fleamarket?" said another girl cattily.

"Yes, I do. But only for myself. That's all I have money left for."

"So why do you send things here, darling?"

"So you won't badmouth me, darling. But you do anyway, I know it. People from Prague write me everything, and the censors let gossip through. In Paris we know everything that goes on."

"You know sweet nothing there!"

"You know sweet nothing *here!*"

The lieutenant, drawn to the conversation against his will once more, shook his round head and asked, "Do the Blazeks have a boarder or anything like that?"

"No, only a granddaughter."

"How old?"

"About six, I think. Her name is Jana. She'll be going to school in the fall."

"An orphan?"

Kopanec grinned wryly. "A state orphan, you might say. I don't know what the official terminology for it is. Her parents quote betrayed their country unquote by escaping when the fraternal assistance brigade arrived. They thought—naively—that there were some international agreements about reuniting families. And who am I to say? Maybe there are. All I know is that the only ones that exist and are adhered to are agreements about shipments of wheat, and maybe pipeline components. There's nothing about the shipment of children. There's no profit in children."

He realized that the lieutenant was not listening.

"I happen to know also," shrilled the girl who had married the Parisian Kraut, "that your old man is sucking up to that whore Balabasova, so they'll at least let him translate some half-assed Russian play under someone else's name!"

"And I happen to know," said the other girl even more shrilly, "that you're two-timing that capitalist husband of yours with your former lover who's now working for Radio Free Europe. And I'll write him about it, you'd better believe it. That much French I do know!"

The lieutenant, though he was thinking about something else, was still astonished at the efficiency of modern communications and at the powerlessness of all the mechanisms and measures designed to eliminate private interests in the name of the state. He came to his feet like a sleepwalker.

"Are you all right?" asked Kopanec, concerned. "Why, you haven't even touched a drop."

The old detective only shook his head. To the tune of the song about dear Augustin, he went out into the hallway.

. . .

"Do you know Jana Blazek?" he said to a boy in a young pioneer's kerchief, who stood by the courtyard pump playing with a yo-yo that displayed a garish portrait of Mickey Mouse.

"Yup."

"Look," said the lieutenant, "I'll give you ten crowns if you'll go to the Blazeks' and ask Jana to come out and play with you."

"Make it Tuzex crowns," said the boy.

The old detective sighed, reached into his pocket, and pulled out a scruffy wallet bearing a picture of the New York skyline. It contained five banknotes of the desired kind, which had been sent to his daughter from Memphis. He had intended to use them in the foreign-currency shop to buy a product called Instant Cocoa for his granddaughter. He gave one to the boy and stuck the wallet, a gift from his son-in-law, back into his pocket.

"One more," said the young pioneer.

Out came the wallet with the picture of New York on it and the little boy got what he asked for. He rolled the bill up, stuck the Mickey Mouse yo-yo into his pocket, and said, "The Blazeks won't let her come out, because it's too late. But I'll try anyway, so you can't say I didn't."

He ran upstairs through the dark corridor.

The lieutenant leaned against the pump and looked at the buildings facing the courtyard. Old baroque houses, once witness to the small, inconsequential human tragedies captured so well by the writer Jan Neruda. The lieutenant had not read Neruda's *Mala Strana Tales* for a long time—not, in fact, since he'd been a student at the Kostelec grammar school. But Neruda's name often came up during political schooling sessions. Jan Neruda had also written an essay on the First of May, and Boruvka's instructors had told him that he was, in fact, a socialist agent. No, they hadn't called him an agent, he corrected himself; that was what someone had called the girl who had married a German Parisian. The writer had merely been a socialist. That was where the difference lay. Perhaps.

He could hear the sound of a phonograph coming from an open window somewhere. His daughter, Zuzana, had the same song in her well-played record collection. She was no longer the same Zuzana who had once, long ago, secretly telephoned Olda Spacek because she couldn't solve an ordinary equation with a single unknown. She was now a mother—and a wife.

Leaning against the pump, the lieutenant could not stop the flow of memories. They were all recent. They had to do with waiting in corridors, spelled off by Mrs. Boruvka, filling out requests, waiting in the outer offices of people he believed could do something. The boy with the yo-yo had reminded him of his vain attempt to bribe a bigwig who promised to help and then reneged with the excuse that there was nothing he could do, which might well have been true. In any case, he didn't return the money. That had been Tuzex currency too, also from Memphis, Tennessee. "Help me, Information," said the lieutenant to himself, for though the record was so worn it was scarcely comprehensible, and though his knowledge of English was scanty, the words had burned themselves into his memory like a magic spell, like a prayer, like a formula of longing, of meager hope and enormous despair. The distant phonograph on the fourth floor was now playing another sad song:

> No matter what the future brings
> I love you more than anything

The lieutenant wiped a tear away with the wide palm of his hand, and fumbled for his handkerchief.

The boy ran out of the dark corridor, his Mickey Mouse yo-yo once again readied for action.

"Jana's not home," he announced.

"And where is she?"

"She went to visit her aunt in Mydloves."

The lieutenant said nothing. He knew the village. It was in the south, close to the West German border. He stared blankly at nothing, unperceiving. The distant phonograph on the fourth floor played on.

> They told me on the way, they
> told me, "Joe
> There's no way she'll be yours again
> no more. . . ."

The boy with the Mickey Mouse yo-yo stared at him in alarm. There were tears streaming down the old man's cheeks. He was still staring at him when the man stumbled through the courtyard gate into the street, where the first gas lamps were just being lit.

. . .

Back at the department, an excited pair was waiting for him. "There's a suspicious bunch at Kopanec's place," he said. "Full of people connected with the Dubcek era."

'Wrong, comrade lieutenant!" Pudil didn't even let him finish. "I don't mean to say you're not right. But this time it wasn't any of them. You'll flip when I tell you what Comrade Malek and I found out at Interior."

The lieutenant abandoned his effort to lead the exemplary young security agent off the track.

"Ever heard the name Joe Bomb?" asked Pudil.

The old detective shook his head.

"I'll bet you haven't. He's a very careful bird, this one. A Czech-American. Left in 1939 when the Nazis came. You get me?"

Despite the weariness he felt come over him, the lieutenant managed a wry smile. "He's a Zionist, you mean."

This surprised the sergeant. "I—jeez, I forgot to check on that. But never mind. There's no time for that now. His name used to be Bambasek, but in the U.S.A. he changed it to Bomb. Anyway, this fellow Bomb has come into the country twice in the last month. Twice! In one month!"

"Kopanec had a loud argument yesterday with Novotny," said the lieutenant weakly. "The whole house heard it."

"Not surprising," said the sergeant, "but irrelevant in this connection. On his first visit, this Joe Bomb fellow dropped in on two people. And now, hang on to your socks!"

The lieutenant had no need to brace himself. He could sense what was coming.

"The first was a woman called Cermak in a place called Mydloves. It's in the Sumava foothills."

'Why?" asked the lieutenant without interest.

"Just hang on. The second visit is really interesting. Blazek!! Novotny's next-door neighbor! And you know why?"

"No," said the lieutenant. "Are they related?"

"That's just it. They're not. But Bomb lives in Pittsburgh. And the Blazeks have a daughter who skipped the country with her husband after the fraternal troops intervened, and they ended up in Pittsburgh!"

"First we thought he was just bringing some family messages," said Malek uneasily. "But the whole thing's a lot more complicated."

The sergeant then began to tell the old detective a story he himself had already partly pieced together while waiting by the pump in the baroque courtyard. The man who had changed his name to Joe Bomb was not related to Mrs. Cermak of Mydloves. But Mrs. Cermak was another daughter of the pensioners who were Novotny's neighbors.

"His first trip here wasn't so suspicious," said Pudil. "But the second one! He arrived three days ago and the first person he meets isn't a relative of his either. Someone called Oldrich Spacek, an aviation engineer who works for Avia. And there's a connection here too that's got nothing to do with family."

The lieutenant felt the shock of sudden panic. He knew the engineer from Avia better than he cared to admit. He became terribly afraid lest Zuzana, whom Oldrich Spacek had once helped out in mathematics and God knows what else, might somehow be dragged into this affair as well.

"Spacek," the sergeant went on, "is a pilot in the Army Aeronautics Club, Svazarm. And Svazarm," he said, grinning, "has an airfield in Mydloves!"

He paused to see what the old detective would say but, when he said nothing, Pudil went on: "I don't suppose it makes any sense to you, does it? Well, I'm not surprised. Because there's a missing link. And that link is called Jana Blazek. She's six years old and she's the daughter of those escapees in Pittsburgh."

"Oh, so that's it," sighed the lieutenant.

"They want to kidnap her, the pirates!" the sergeant shouted. "But they've counted their chickens too soon. Public Security in

Mydloves has already been given the alarm. They'll let us know the minute Joe Bomb shows up there with the girl!" He calmed down somewhat and added, "Oh, I almost forgot to tell you. On this second trip, Joe Bomb drove in with his own car from West Germany, a Pontiac."

"Are you sure about all this?" said the lieutenant. "Did you confirm that the girl has actually left Prague?"

"That wasn't necessary, comrade," said the sergeant, and then, still stinging from the recent unprecedented reprimand, added quickly, "Comrade lieutenant, Comrade Novotny was asked to keep track of what went on at the Blazeks. And Comrade Novotny died at the hand of a murderer. A murderer who knew karate."

"He obviously tried to restrain Bomb," Malek piped up timidly, "and paid the consequences. We'll call Interior in on this, won't we? I mean, it goes beyond our mandate now."

"Wait a minute!" the lieutenant intervened, standing up. "Don't call anywhere."

"Why not?"

"This does not go beyond our mandate," declared the lieutenant in a mournful voice. "Bomb is a . . . a murderer," he said wearily. "He killed Novotny. And that's our job—to catch murderers."

"But this is a clear case of air piracy!" objected the sergeant.

"That is the intent," said the lieutenant. "So far, though, only the crime of murder has actually been committed. And that falls within our mandate."

"I don't know, Josef," said Malek. "The comrades from Interior certainly wouldn't mind making the arrests for us. Even though it's debatable who should do what."

"Of course they wouldn't mind," said the lieutenant. "But we're bound by an oath. It's our *responsibility* to do everything in our power to arrest *anyone* who commits murder." Out of the corner of his eye, he saw the sergeant's face, which showed signs of an inner struggle. He resorted to a dishonorable ruse: "And then, comrades," he said, in a voice that sounded unnatural to his own ears, though they may have been oversensitive, "haven't you got just a little ambition? Aren't you even slightly proud to belong to a unit that is about to capture a criminal who not only murdered a comrade, but is getting ready to kidnap a *Czech* child and spirit her away to the West?"

"I think the main issue here is cooperation between the different branches," Malek objected feebly. The lieutenant, however, experienced a sensation of fleeting triumph, for the sergeant went for the bait.

"That's a fact, all right," Pudil declared. "We might even look at it as a kind of socialist competition. The murderer is ours, the air pirates belong to the comrades from Interior, as long as no weapons are used. But that's their problem, isn't it? If they're not vigilant and alert enough to come to the correct conclusions by themselves, why should we pass the ball to them when we can score the goal ourselves and at the same time stop those birds from flying the coop?"

"Let's go then," said Lieutenant Boruvka.

And they went.

. . .

They went. The lieutenant didn't even have time to say goodbye to Zuzana and his wife. He merely called to tell them he wouldn't be home that night, which was nothing unusual in the old detective's family. And then they went. Down a long highway undulating across hilltops beneath the stars, winding among silvery-green meadows that sparkled with diamond dew. A large moon hung over the countryside, as round as the lieutenant's face and, that night, just as pale. As pale as a white skull. Not the one from Edgar Allan Poe's fantasy, but one from the lieutenant's own experience. They drove past wheatfields golden in the daytime, the color of gold now, at night, waving in the night breeze beneath the cherry trees that lined the road. They drove through woods where the black shadows of magnificent owls flitted among the trees. A moth landed on the lieutenant's nose, then flew away; the sergeant, hunched over the wheel of the Volga, pushed the motor to the limit and the lieutenant's loaded pistol dug into his hip. The countryside sped by the open windows, redolent of barns and manure piles, villages submerged in darkness and silence, a landscape of clover and alfalfa, the lieutenant's landscape, with ponds reflecting a twisted moon, like the crumpled collages of one of those artists from the Dubcek era who later committed suicide— an ordinary suicide from an era of normalization. A landscape of fireflies and old, ancient history, a countryside where criminals were drawn and quartered at a time when the city of Memphis no longer existed and did not yet exist. A large vampire bat dipped across the stars. They stopped for a piss, as the sergeant put it. They urinated into a ditch at the side of the road where purple thistles grew; a large family of hedgehogs filed across the road, the lieutenant said his farewells, and they got back into the car.

Again they drove, rising and descending, along the narrow highway, along the umbilical cord of life, soon to be severed. The landscape smelled of darkness, of stars, of spruce trees, of ponds, of old-fashioned train stations, of the moon—and they were silent, the landscape possessed by darkness. Some lines of poetry surfaced in the lieutenant's aching mind and they had a meaning, though he did not know what; he only sensed it was bad. Memories tempting him back into the saddle, that procession from his past, the girls with the bloody breasts who, it was decided in higher places, had been murdered by an unknown assailant, the dancer with the sad slippers with a hopeless four-leaf clover clinging to them who, it was decided in higher places, had died of accidental asphyxiation by natural gas. And what, then, do those higher places leave in hands other than their own? Nothing? We needn't be here at all, then. The foolish, wizened little informer killed by a karate blow to the neck, humiliated people who trustingly accept an offer of new pride, the receding landscape, trees pregnant with fruit swaying above the lurching Volga. . . . The lieutenant caught his head in his hands and said to Malek, "Pavel, you don't happen to have an aspirin with you, by any chance?"

· · ·

At four in the morning they drove into Resetice. The lieutenant phoned Mydloves from the police station. The local cop, who hadn't slept all night, confirmed that Bomb had arrived at the Cermaks' before midnight and carried the sleeping girl out of his car. The old detective issued the appropriate orders, then they left the Volga in Resetice and set off on foot down an overgrown track through the fields for the Mydloves airfield, about four kilometers away. It was getting light. A pale sliver on the eastern horizon slowly flared, expanded, and golden rays of light from the still-hidden sun shot through the pink clouds. At 5:30 they reached the airfield. It was a flat, uplands meadow, the grass cut short, with a narrow strip of concrete, an air sock, and, at the end of the runway, a wooden hangar. They knocked. The sleepy cop from Mydloves greeted them in the doorway.

"Nothing so far," he whispered. "They haven't shown up yet." The lieutenant went inside and peered through a small window. Beyond the airfield the land fell away towards the village, beige and white in the early morning light. Above the village stood the white tower of a little church, topped with a red onion dome. A flock of quail flew out of the field, a swallow dipped and swirled over the meadow flushed pink with clover blossoms. A rooster crowed in the village, driving off death. Cows mooed. They heard an urban droning sound.

"Careful," whispered Pudil, standing behind the lieutenant. There was a faint click as he disengaged the safety catch on his weapon. The local cop looked nervously at him and then squinted at the lieutenant.

"Are we going to use guns?"

"Not you, under any circumstances," said the lieutenant. "This is our business."

The sound grew louder and a car appeared on the narrow track through the field. It was a big, beige, two-tone American Pontiac, with a coffee-colored roof, lurching along the path like a drunken ship. It stopped at the edge of the narrow concrete runway. An enormous man in a wide-brimmed hat stepped out and looked at his watch. He was tall, like the hero in a cowboy movie. The sun, just edging over the horizon, shone on his head. The man looked around and the lieutenant saw a bronzed, creased face that reminded him of illustrations in the old novels by Cooper he'd read as a child.

"Bomb!" whispered the sergeant.

The lieutenant merely nodded.

The man glanced at his watch again, then leaned over to say something to someone in the car. In the window of the Pontiac was the silhouette of a woman in a babushka. The man stepped away from the car, positioned himself at the end of the concrete runway, and stood with his legs apart.

The sun came up, the pink clouds faded to white, the fields on the opposite hillside sparkled gold. It was silent except for the chirping of awakening crickets and the chatter of birds. The swallow was performing low-level acrobatics again over the runway.

Then they heard another faint droning sound. The enormous man tipped his hat farther down his forehead to shade his eyes from the rising sun. The droning increased; a dot appeared in the blue sky and grew until it was recognizable as a small, blue airplane. The man raised both hands. The plane banked, then leveled and began its approach, pointing its nose straight at the end of the runway. It descended, flared, its wheels touched the concrete. The man remained with his arms outstretched while the plane taxied up to him. Then he ran to the car. The aircraft came to a halt, someone inside threw back the bubble canopy, and the head of a young man in a flying helmet appeared. The lieutenant recognized him.

But still he remained silent.

"Comrade lieutenant! Let's nail 'em," whispered Sergeant Pudil nervously.

The old detective gave out a sound like a groan, but Sergeant Pudil interpreted it in his own way. Briskly he threw open the hangar door and, with his pistol drawn, ran out onto the airfield. The man in the wide-brimmed hat, with the little girl in his arms, was just turning around. He saw the sergeant and started running towards the plane in long, loping strides.

"Halt!" roared the sergeant. The plane began turning around. "You too!" The sergeant pointed to the pilot with his left hand. "One move and I'll shoot you all! Comrade lieutenant!"

Malek ran out of the hangar and slowly, almost embarrassedly, pulled out his pistol. He looked around at the lieutenant.

"You take care of the pilot," the sergeant shrieked at Malek, "and you, put that kid down!"

The man in the wide-brimmed hat stopped, hesitated.

"Make it snappy or I'll shoot! Comrade lieutenant, where are you?"

In the hangar, Lieutenant Boruvka came to his senses. He looked around and saw the village cop standing there awkwardly. Several buttons on his shirt were undone. The lieutenant drew his pistol and pointed it at him.

"Give me your pistol," he commanded. "Come on! That's an order!"

The policeman fumbled with his holster and uncertainly handed the lieutenant his gun.

The old detective walked out of the hangar. The sergeant looked round at him and said, less loudly now, "Good! You cover him while I search him for weapons, comrade lieutenant." He stuck his own pistol into his holster and walked up to the man in the wide-brimmed hat.

"Stay where you are," said the lieutenant. His voice was scarcely audible. Sergeant Pudil stopped abruptly, then looked around in alarm, as though he'd been caught off guard by someone else entering the game.

"Yes, you," said the lieutenant, aiming the pistol in his right hand at the sergeant's chest. "And you, Pavel, throw down your gun," he told Malek, aiming the second pistol at him.

"Josef, come on," said Malek uncertainly.

The sergeant stared from one to the other in astonishment. Then he shouted at Malek, "Shoot! This is sabotage!"

"Come on, Josef, don't be crazy," said Malek nervously.

"I'm not crazy, Pavel. I'm deadly serious. Throw down your gun."

The man in the wide-brimmed hat watched everything with dangerously calm eyes.

"Get serious, Josef. You can't . . ."

"I will if . . . if I have to, Pavel. Please don't make me. . . ."

Slowly, Lieutenant Malek let his arm fall and dropped the pistol into the grass. The old detective knew—and it warmed his heart for an instant—that Malek hadn't done it because he feared for his life. The enormous man's eyes flashed. He bent down quickly, grabbed the child, who had begun to cry, and was at the plane in several long strides. The young man in the flying helmet leaned out of the cockpit and lifted the child inside.

"Quick!" the man called to the lieutenant. "Come on! It's a two-seater. There's room for two *and* the kid."

The lieutenant shook his head. "You get in!"

"No, you go. Give me the guns. I can look after myself!"

Once more the lieutenant shook his head. "No you can't. Get in! There's not much time!"

"You're risking your neck, man!"

"So are you," said the lieutenant. "And my family still lives here."

The man in the wide-brimmed hat hesitated a moment longer. His bronzed face, creased with the marks of a different, more violent experience than the lieutenant's, was lit by the morning sun.

"Get a move on!" said the old detective.

For another brief moment the man looked at the Pontiac where the country woman with the kerchief on her head sat shyly, then back at the lieutenant. "Okay," he said. "Good luck, pardner."

He swung himself up into the cockpit. The plexiglas canopy snapped shut, the engine roared as the plane swung round and accelerated along the concrete runway. It lurched heavily into the air and rose slowly over the field of clover towards the west. They could see it a while longer, then it dipped over the woods and was gone.

The sergeant let his hands fall. "I can't believe this. . . ."

"Keep your hands up," said the lieutenant. "We have to wait at least a half an hour. It's thirty kilometers to the border. I hope they fly low enough to avoid the radar." Then he grinned. It was a sad grin, without a trace of irony. "Just like those Zionists. Remember, Pudil!"

. . .

The young—or rather, not so young, but still attractive—blonde woman in bell-bottomed trousers and a honey-colored sweater stood respectfully in front of an overweight man who slouched in a chair behind his desk, picking at his teeth with a toothpick.

"No, we're not related," she was saying, "but we were friends for many years. That counts for something, doesn't it?"

"Only immediate family have the right to a visit. Wives, children . . ."

"His wife died when—when it happened. She had a stroke."

"Does that surprise you, comrade?" said the man, examining a piece of meat he had pried out of his teeth.

"No, it doesn't. But the fact is, she died and we . . . we were planning to get married."

The man looked at her derisively. "That's not something I'd go around advertising. She died after they arrested him."

"What I mean to say is," said the blonde woman, "that I'd like to marry him. If that's possible."

"It's not," said the man, "and it won't be for another fifteen years. And anyway, who knows," he went on, looking her up and down, "if you'll still want to marry him then. He'll be sixty-seven when he gets out."

The blonde pouted contemptuously.

"Unless he keeps his nose clean," said the man, "and there's a political amnesty. But don't hold your breath. It's going to take us some time to clean up the moral havoc wreaked by people like him."

"He didn't wreak any moral havoc."

"He aided and abetted an act of air piracy," said the man. "And he was lucky he did it before the National Assembly brought back the rope. Otherwise—" he grinned insolently "—you wouldn't be able to marry him, not even when you turn," and again he ran his eyes over the woman's trim figure, "fifty or whatever."

"A hundred and fifty," said the blonde, returning his insolent sneer. "So you won't let me see him?"

"Out of the question," said the man. "Who do you think you are? The law applies to everyone. You're wasting my time."

He looked directly into her eyes. She stared back at him defiantly.

"Unless," said the man, and he looked around, took his phone off the hook, and lowered his voice, "unless some exceptional reasons were offered. Do you know what I mean?" He ran his eyes over her again, from the bell-bottomed trousers, up her slender thighs and her shapely breasts, to her large mouth and gray eyes.

The blonde woman looked at him disdainfully. "In that case, I'd just as soon forget about it, even though it tears my heart out. If you know what a heart is."

The man lowered his voice even more. "Come on, lady! Surely it's worth two grand, isn't it? Or are you going to stand there and tell me you'll wait fifteen years? You're no spring chicken yourself."

. . .

The woman was uncertain whether it had really been worth the two grand, which took a hefty slice out of her modest savings. The lieutenant—of course he was a lieutenant no longer—was brought into the large, gray, unpleasant visiting room. They sat him down opposite her, with a thick wire mesh between them. The old detective was wearing clothes made of the kind of cloth they make cheap rugs from. She had feared the encounter, but was encouraged when she saw that the lieutenant's round face had not aged. On the contrary, it almost seemed to her that it had grown younger. In any case, it was calm. The blue eyes looked at her through the wire mesh, and a deep, tender friendship radiated from them.

Like everyone else in this situation, they didn't know what to talk about, so they merely chatted. The lieutenant told her how much he regretted the fact that Malek had been demoted to constable for not using his weapon, though they hadn't discharged him because he had claimed that he simply couldn't believe his eyes, and they had treated that as an extenuating circumstance. The sergeant was promoted to first lieutenant. The Blazeks, out of consideration for their advanced age, were sentenced to three years each, and Mrs. Cermak and her husband got five. Joe Bomb was given the noose in absentia and the state prosecutor requested his extradition from the United States. The request was turned down. So they confiscated the Pontiac. In the glove compartment they found an American Express card, and this led Pudil off on a long wild-goose chase through the archives of the Ministry of the Interior, but he never did manage to find even a trace of Zionism clinging to the name Bambasek.

Then the singer spoke. She had managed to make a kind of comeback. A certain Kopanec, a writer who, though blacklisted, still had influential contacts, had written a television program about her under the pseudonym of a trusted Party member. The program had gone down well, and now she was touring with Vaclav Hybs's group, mainly to Bulgaria, the Soviet Union, and occasionally Cuba. Perhaps one day they'd go to Chile too. She saw that the lieutenant was pleased by the news, but then he grew sad. Cuba, he said. That was almost in America. "And they've definitely turned down Zuzana's application to leave," he said. "But you know how it is, Eve. Her husband's in the States. In Memphis, Tennessee. That's what makes me feel worst of all. You know how it is. She's my daughter."

. . .

"Poor Dad," said Zuzana. They were sitting by an open window; it was the month when cats make love and the velvet cavaliers, suspecting nothing about the world and its changeable laws, sang their unchanging song across the tile rooftops. "I can tell you now, Eve. I know you and Father were having an affair, but it doesn't bother me. Perhaps there's some kind of cosmic justice in it."

"I'm ashamed," said the blonde. "But you know yourself how helpless you can feel in a situation like that."

"I do," said Zuzana. "Did you know he's not my real father?"

The blonde woman was astonished. "You're kidding!"

"See my eyes?" said Zuzana, opening her very pretty green eyes for the singer to see.

"Yes?"

"And have you noticed what color father's eyes are?"

"Of course," said the blonde. "Forget-me-not blue."

"And mother's were gray."

"And?"

"So practically speaking, it's impossible," said Zuzana. "A blue-eyed man and a gray-eyed woman, if they stood on their heads, could never give birth to a creature like me."

Both women were silent. On the rooftops, the eternal tomcats sang their song.

"But he's my father all the same," said Zuzana. "I couldn't have had a better one. Even though in the end he . . . no, he didn't screw up. Father didn't screw anything up. It was the others who did that—the bastards!"

. . .

They lay in each other's arms, the blonde woman and the girl with green eyes, and they wept until the moon came out and the tomcats fell silent.

"Can I stay the night?" asked the blonde woman.

"Sure. We'll sleep here in my parents' bed."

Lying beside each other and staring into the darkness, the blonde said, "He told me—when we were saying goodbye—something very strange. I don't understand what he meant."

"What was it?"

"He said that no matter how it was and no matter whether he did a good thing or not, he said, at least some fish or other died. From the Paraná River. Do you know what he was talking about?"

"No, I don't," said Zuzana. "He never told me anything like that."

They stared into the darkness for a long time. Then they fell asleep. On the other side of the city, the former lieutenant slept on a wooden cot, sleeping the deep, dreamless sleep of people who, though they may be misguided, are kind and honorable.